Noel of Sin © 2024 Jodie King All rights reserved.

The characters and events depicted in this book are entirely fictitious. Names, characters, settings, and incidents are either created by the author's imagination or utilized fictitiously. Any resemblance to a living or deceased person, event, or location is completely coincidental.

Except for brief quotations in a book review, no part of this book may be duplicated or reproduced in any form or by any method, whether electronic or mechanical, including photocopying, recording, or by any information storage and collection system, without the author's written permission.

For more information on the author and her books, visit her linktree**: https://linktr.ee/Jodie_King_Author**

For the full list of **trigger and content warnings,** please scan this QR code, where you will be taken directly to my website:

or you can visit my website by clicking here -

www.JodieKingAuthor.com

Authors note: These warnings are laid bare; It's now entirely your choice whether to read this book or not. Please take every single warning with seriousness and beyond.

Your mental health matters.

Dedication

This Christmas, we're throwing the nice list in the fucking fire and making the naughty list look like a damn invitation. Forget adorable carols, mistletoe kisses and cosy traditions. Stockings won't be hung by the chimney; they'll be torn and tossed the fuck aside. This is the kind of forbidden that burns hotter than any Yule log.

By the end of this, even Christmas lights will make you feel ashamed and snowflakes won't melt nearly as fast as your composure. So tell me... are you ready to sin a little harder for Rook this holiday season? I can't promise you'll ever make it back on that nice list again.

But the risk is so, so worth it.

CHAPTER ONE

Stepping out of the car, I tilt my head back, straining my neck to take in the towering skyscraper looming in front of me. My eyes trace its sharp lines, disappearing into the night sky as delicate flakes of snow kiss my freshly made-up face.

I close my eyes for a moment, drawing in a long, cold breath. When I finally look ahead, the entrance glows—a grand arch of twinkling Christmas lights drapes over the double doors like a false hope of warmth inside. Boston on Christmas Eve, another family get together. We do this every year, sometimes at the Lakehouse cabin or a different location. This time, my stepmom chose this place, no doubt with my dad's wallet to back it.

For the past few years, this season has felt like the tightening of a noose around my neck, each year a reminder that I might have to face him again. My stepbrother. Rook. My pulse quickens at the thought of his voice—menacing, careless, capable of ripping me apart in a matter of seconds.

My Christmas's have always belonged to him. From those perfect childhood memories, when he was both my protector and my tormentor, to that dark, forbidden Christmas two years ago. The night everything shattered. The night we broke everything we were.

Maybe he won't be here this year—just like last year. Maybe he'll remain a ghost, haunting me only in the shadows of my mind. We were torn apart after that night, ripped from the wreckage we'd made. My father took Rook away, banished him to somewhere I couldn't follow, and since then, I haven't seen him. Not once. I've not even had a text.

Still, I know he's not dead. If he were, his mom would've killed my dad by now or at least tried to. Losing him felt like losing a vital organ—a part of me I can't live without but somehow must. Those final words I hurled at him, sharp as daggers, still echo in my mind. I remember the hurt in his teary eyes, the way I broke something inside him. But I had no choice. I told myself it had to be this way. I still tell myself that. And yet, the wound of it hasn't healed. I'm not sure it ever will.

With a sharp slam, I shut the car door behind me. My fingers shake as I smooth out the tight, glittering black dress that clings to my skin, the cold seeping through the fabric. I wrap my dark grey, cropped faux fur jacket closer, but it does little to guard me against the bite of the icy air. The snowfall thickens, each flake heavier than the last, and for a moment, I hesitate.

This Christmas feels... Different.

After bracing myself, I push past the dread coiling in my chest and force my feet to move toward the glowing doors, my heels crunching over the thick snow.

Once inside, I brush the snow from my shoulders and step into the quiet, lavishly decorated reception. It's eerily empty, the festive garlands and twinkling lights doing little to mask the stillness that comes with Christmas Eve this late. I imagine most of the staff are home, huddled with their families, drinking hot cocoa. My heels click softly across the polished floor as I approach the elevator. Without hesitation, I press the button for the penthouse—the top floor, where my family waits.

As the elevator takes its time, I mentally rehearse the night's plan: go in, smile, mingle for an hour or two, then leave. Head across the city to Blaise, the guy I'm dating. He's working late, but I plan to meet him at his place for dinner. These nights are like rituals in my family—unavoidable, suffocating traditions. The older I get, the more I hate them, yet with a family like mine, refusing isn't an option. The cost of saying no is always too high.

My dad rules Phantom Syndicate MC with an iron fist here in Boston, his name whispered in shadows like a curse. Ruthless, unruly, and utterly horrifying, he's built his empire on blood and fear. But when it comes to family, his rules are carved in stone—hard and final. As the head of the most notorious motorcycle club in the state and having ties to the mafia, he's a man no one dares to cross. And those poor, stupid souls who even think of stepping out of line? They don't live to regret it.

A soft chime announces the arrival of the elevator, and as the doors glide open, I step inside, my stomach twisting with familiar anxiety. I press the button again, staring at my reflection in the mirror as the doors begin to close. My sleek, long black hair falls perfectly over my shoulders, and I smooth it down with my palm, making sure not even a strand is out of place.

Just as the door is about to seal shut, a hand shoots through the gap, fingers curling around the edge, stopping the cold metal in its tracks. My heart stutters, every beat uneven as I turn slowly. The elevator creaks open wider until I see him and my breath catches in my throat, my lungs forgetting how to function. My eyes immediately lock onto the matte black helmet covering his face. I know it's him, even without seeing him. I can feel it in the way the air shifts; always dense and charged.

Fuck, he's here.

It feels like it's been an eternity since I last saw my big brother.

I notice the fresh ink—new tattoos, black art snaking up his neck like sharp whispers of his madness, a map of the insanity that runs through his veins. Even in this luxurious building, Rook doesn't belong. He never does. Standing in the doorway, his aura carves a hole through the room, impossible to ignore. He doesn't fit. Not in that black tank top, tight black jeans and his leather jacket hanging loose over his frame, looking like he's just stepped out of hell and didn't bother to change. He never gave a shit about blending in, never cared about impressing anyone. He wears what the fuck he wants, because he can.

I can feel him staring at me from behind his tinted visor for a second longer until he steps inside, and I quickly look away, my throat tightening as I swallow hard. I keep my gaze at the corner of my vision as he turns his back to me, and with the soft hiss of the doors closing, I let my eyes trail up his towering frame. Rook stands at 6'7", dwarfing my 5'4", and I've always hated how small I feel around him. But now, he seems so much taller.

I notice his posture is rigid, while he looks ahead, as if I'm not even here and the ignorance hits me in the chest, a sting I wasn't really prepared for. A sharp, unexpected sorrow pierces through me, but I fight to keep it locked away. I want to say something, anything, but the silence between us is loud enough to fill the whole elevator. It's clear now—he doesn't want to talk to me. Not yet. Not ever, maybe.

The sister in me wants to reach out, ask how he's been, maybe wrap my arms around him and pretend none of this ever happened. But the other part of me—the one responsible for breaking everything—reminds me to stay quiet, to just leave him alone. He doesn't need me. It's for the best.

After what feels like forever, the elevator finally stops and the door swipes open. In the distance, I hear Christmas music and people talking, but Rook doesn't move. He stands like a fucking monster blocking my path. I wait, until finally, he walks forward, entering the annoying family gathering.

I let out a tense breath, needing a strong drink after this. I watch him until he disappears out of view, then I finally leave the elevator as well, straightening my shoulders as I stride toward the noise and music.

When I step into the lavish living room, decked in black, gold and red like some holiday postcard, my gaze drifts to the open kitchen on the right. That's where everyone is, laughing too loud, sipping too much, the drinks flowing freely. I hesitate at the threshold, watching from the shadows as Rook makes his entrance.

He doesn't need to say anything—just his presence shifts the entire vibe in the room. My dad gives him a nod, stiff and forced, barely masking the tension simmering beneath.

They've never gotten along. My dad raised Rook since he was twelve, but it's always been a battlefield, not a bond. Rook's real father was the head of the Sinister Stalkers MC, the same rival club my dad spent years trying to crush. When Rook's dad died, instead of carrying on the club, his mom did the unthinkable—she married my dad, the enemy.

Do they love each other? In some twisted way, I think so. They've found something strong, maybe even genuine, amidst all the heartaches. She's been good to me, but with Rook and my dad, it's different. The past clings to them like smoke, choking out any chance of peace.

Rook has never wanted this life, never wanted the expectations my dad dumped on him. Taking a role in the club that tore his father's apart? It's a betrayal he can't stomach. I think he believes all the time he's against the idea of being obedient to my dad, he isn't deceiving his own, even from beyond the grave, which, strangely, I understand.

My dad, on the other hand, sees Rook as a liability—a loose end that needs tying. The air between them feels volatile, like a lit match too close to gasoline. I stay frozen at the edge of the room, watching, waiting, just like every other time I've been in the same space as them. It's like a ticking time bomb. Even more so now and I feel uncomfortable.

Over the years, his mom has stopped my dad from killing him more times than I can count. And, just as often, she's kept Rook from doing the same to my dad. Their hatred is repeated, a savage tug-of-war that never breaks but never ends. Rook was always unruly, brutal in his own right—a born leader who refused to bow to anyone, least of all my dad. He never saw him as a father, never even pretended. And that? That boldness was a constant source of chaos. Fights that shook the walls, words sharp enough to draw blood.

I know how hard my dad can be. I've been on the receiving end of his strict shit far too many times. For me, it's simpler, but no less suffocating. I was supposed to be the perfect MC princess. Stay out of trouble. Look pretty. Keep myself intact, pure and untouched, until I'm handed off like a prize to a husband within the biker family. It doesn't matter who, as long as they're one of us.

I've seen what happens when someone challenges my father's rules. The aftermath isn't something you forget. So, I toe the line. Smile when I'm supposed to. Hide the cracks beneath the surface. Rook? He was never one to hide. And my dad doesn't forgive rebellion. Not from anyone. Not even his own family.

That Christmas was proof of that. Rook… I… We crossed a line that almost got us both killed and tore this family apart. That night humiliated me. I couldn't sleep for months after, couldn't stop thinking about what we did, and I'm only just feeling like I'm starting to move on from it. But for the first time in two years, we're only now allowed in the same breathing space as one another, and I can feel it all over me. It's all crashing down around me with every inhale.

I wonder where he's been or where my dad forced him to go. The question won't leave me alone, gnawing at the edges of my mind, but deep down, I know it weren't good. I want to ask him. God, I want to talk to him so badly. But I can't. I shouldn't. Things aren't the same between us anymore.

He's not my big brother.

He's… something else.

Something forbidden.

Something I shouldn't even be thinking about.

But it wasn't just about me or what I felt. It was about Rook. Two years ago, he put me in an impossible position. He asked me to leave with him. To be with him. Not as his sister—as something more. I told him no, in a harsh way. Harsher than it should have been.

Words spilled from my lips like poison. Words I can never take back. Not because I didn't want to leave with him. Deep down, I did. I wanted to leave this prison of a life behind, but I was just... so fucking confused. One minute he was my big brother, my entire world, but the next he was looking at me like I was the only thing that mattered, the only thing he could ever love, asking me to break every rule we'd ever lived by.

He thought it could work; thought we could just run and leave all of this behind. But I knew better. My dad would never let it slide. He's far too powerful. He wouldn't just send Rook away. He'd make sure Rook was gone—for good. Dead. He wouldn't give a shit what his wife had to say. When my dad see's red, it's game over. Everything else comes after.

And I couldn't let that happen.

If I said yes, I wouldn't just lose Rook for a while. I'd lose him forever. I wouldn't see him at Christmas or hear his voice again. So, I made the only choice I could. I shut him out. Cut him off. I hurt him. I didn't choose him.

I hope one day he can get past the damage and forgive me. I wish we could rewind and change everything that shattered us. I miss him so fucking much.

After some time of lingering at the archway, I force myself to move. The sharp click of my tall heels against the glittering black tiles cuts through the hum of conversation, drawing every eye.

Except his.

Rook is still facing away, one hand gripping the edge of the counter as he pulls off his helmet with the other. I catch the tousle of his dark brown hair beneath it, but I tear my gaze away, forcing myself to look at my dad who's watching me closely, too closely. His stance is tense, his expression unreadable and cold, but I can feel the tension rolling off him in waves.

When I reach him, he stretches a big, tattooed arm out, tucking me against him in a way that feels more suffocatingly protective than affectionate as his lips press against my forehead.

"Merry Christmas, princess," he murmurs low.

I force a tight smile, the words tasting strange on my tongue as I reply, "Merry Christmas, Dad."

But I can't stop my attention moving back to Rook. He hasn't turned, his broad back to me as he leans casually against the counter, talking quietly to our cousin, Jack. His voice rumbles, low and smooth, the kind that makes the room feel smaller, heavier. Then he moves, sweeping his tattooed fingers through his long, dark strands and the sight shouldn't make my stomach flip, shouldn't make my throat feel like it's closing, but it does.

Get it together, I tell myself. I curl my fingers into fists at my sides, willing myself to calm down. But the harder I try to pull myself together, the more I realize I'm unraveling, piece by piece.

"No Blaise tonight?" my dad asks, his voice cutting through the room loud enough for everyone to hear.

My body tenses, stiffening like I've been caught doing something wrong. The mention of him makes me uneasy, but in front of Rook? That's a whole other storm waiting to happen.

I don't know if Rook knows about Blaise, but the way his head turns slightly at the name tells me he's paying attention now. My stomach tightens, anxiety clawing at me. Rook's never handled the idea of me being with someone else—he's always been jealous, possessive, unhinged even, making people disappear or hurt. The thought of me being forced into something I don't want, or worse, with someone who isn't him, has always set him off in ways that makes him seem insane.

Blaise is from a smaller biker gang in the city, not even close to ours in power or reputation. But they've always been on good terms with my dad, and a couple of months ago, my dad decided it was time to start parading me around, setting me up with men who met his standards. Blaise stuck. Not because I wanted him to, but because it kept my dad off my back.

And now? Things are… comfortable. Not love. Not even close. But it's something that's manageable. Something that keeps my dad from pushing harder. Or so I thought.

I drop my eyes, my fingers twisting at the soft fur on my sleeve as I mumble, "No, he's working late."

The words feel heavy in my mouth, and I keep my gaze fixed on some meaningless point in the distance, avoiding everyone's eyes.

"That's a shame, I would have liked to have seen my son in law on Christmas Eve."

My eyes close, the unease creeping up my spine and when I open them again, I notice Rook's jaw ticks, the muscle flexing in distain before he looks forward again. My dad's already pushing stupid buttons, wanting a reaction. We've been here for two fucking minutes.

15

I inhale deeply and look up at my dad, offering a small, passive smile, "Let's not get ahead of ourselves, Daddy. We're not married."

My dad raises a brow, assessing my attitude carefully, but I don't break eye contact, I stand my ground, making it known that this is my choice, it always will be, no matter how much he breathes down my neck with his bullshit controlling ways.

"Yet," he retorts firmly, and I fight the urge to roll my eyes.

Suddenly, Cindy steps into view, her smile warm but tinged with a nervous energy as she offers me a glass of champagne.

"It's great to see you, Eb. Merry Christmas," she says softly.

I force my gaze away from my dad's, letting the tension between us dissolve just enough and as I take the glass from her, I manage another polite smile. "You too, Cindy."

She pulls me into a tight hug, the kind that feels like she's holding on for a moment too long, before guiding me toward the living room. We settle onto the sleek black couches, the hum of conversation in the kitchen fading into the background.

"I have something for you," she says, reaching into her bag. Her hand trembles as she pulls out a black gift box, tied neatly with a silver ribbon.

My brows pinch together as I take it. She looks at me like she's waiting for something—acceptance, approval, forgiveness. I can't tell which.

I tug at the ribbon, letting it fall away before lifting the lid. Inside is a delicate silver necklace, the diamond pendant glinting softly in the warm light.

"Oh, Cind, I didn't…"

"It's fine," she cuts me off with a dismissive wave, her laugh a little forced. "Do you like it?" she asks, her green eyes locked on mine, searching for something.

I glance back down at the necklace, running my fingers over the cool metal. "I love it. It's beautiful," I say, my voice soft.

She lets out a shaky breath, her tension easing slightly, though it doesn't fully disappear. Cindy's always carried this weight, a shadow of something darker that never quite leaves her. Her past is no secret. When Rook's dad died, she spiraled—drowning in alcohol and men, slipping into a darkness that nearly consumed her. Rook had to fend for himself most of the time, scraping by while she numbed herself to everything. Survival, I guess. Everyone copes in their own way, and who the hell am I to judge?

But then my dad stepped in, and somehow, Cindy found her footing again. My dad might be an asshole, but he's relentless about one thing: structure. He demands order, forces it, and in a twisted way, it saved her. She sobered up, found stability. Maybe even happiness, if you could call it that.

Still, sometimes when I look at her, I see the flaws. The parts of her that never quite healed, that are held together with sheer willpower. And now, sitting here, with her anxious smile and jittery hands, I wonder if this gift is another way she's trying to prove something—to herself, to me, maybe even to Rook.

To ease her tension, I wrap my arms around her tightly, pulling against me in a squeeze. "Love you, Cind." I whisper into her brown hair.

I feel her melt against me before we break apart and when we do, I notice Rook heading this way from the corner of my eye. I look down at the gift box in my lap, carefully placing the lid back on. I don't look up. I can't. Not yet. But I peek through my lashes.

He claims the couch directly across from us, collapsing into it with that infuriating, effortless confidence that's so uniquely his. One arm sprawls over the back, his other hand gripping a beer bottle that sits lazily between his tattooed fingers, perched on his thigh. His long legs part wide, and even though his posture is casual, it's the kind of casual that screams he's in control.

He doesn't speak, doesn't move. But he's staring straight at me. I can feel it. The heaviness of his gaze settles over me like a gloomy shroud. My skin tingles under its intensity, a silent demand that I should look at him. A fucking dare.

He's not avoiding me anymore. He's here to make me squirm, and he's not bothering to hide it. Cindy notices it too and I feel her stiffen beside me, her shift in mood clear.

"Rook…" she says, her voice low, a subtle warning laced in her tone.

He doesn't respond. Doesn't even acknowledge her.

I force myself to meet his eyes, lifting my gaze, cautiously.

But it's a mistake.

The moment our eyes lock, my world spins. His light green stare pierces straight through me, so sharp it feels like it's cutting me open. There's nothing soft left in him—no warmth, no cheeky smile. Just something cold and dangerous lurking behind those darkened orbs.

Two years. That's all it's been, but it feels like a lifetime. He's changed so much, yet in some fucked-up way, he's only become… hotter. It's irritating. My stepbrother has always been attractive—unfortunately—but this? This is something else entirely.

Long gone is the arrogant boy with too much attitude and not enough responsibility to back it up. Now, sitting right in front of me, he's every inch of a man.

He's breathtaking. And I fucking hate it.

His dark, wavy hair, tousled in an effortless way, falls messily across his forehead, brushing his eyes. I notice the black plugs in his earlobes—small, simple, but still enough to remind me he's not the same boy I grew up with. Two hoops sit on either side of his bottom lip, like a viper. He also has a strange small piece of black tape just under his right eye, which confuses me, but it's not even his hair, the piercings, his tanned skin, the thick brows and lashes or the shadow of stubble across his sharp jawline that unsettles me.

It's his eyes.

They're hollowed now with dark circles beneath them that make him look older, harder. But it's not exhaustion. It's something else. Whatever he's seen, whatever he's done, whatever my dad has shown him—it's changed him. The overbearing tension between us is draining the life out of the room, out of me and Cindy clears her throat beside me, trying to break the spell.

"Rook, not when Ryker's here, please," Cindy pleads, and the mention of my dad's name pulls me back to reality.

Rook's eyes slide down my frame, gradually and linger far too long on my bare legs. Then his gaze snaps up to Cindy, his jaw tightening. His head tilts slightly to the side, a subtle challenge in the narrowing of his eyes.

"Am I not allowed to look at or be near my little sister now?" he asks, voice deep and laced with spite. "I mean, you brought this shitshow of a family together, right?"

Little sister.

The words hit me, echoing in my mind. Am I really? After everything? After what we—no. Is this his way of moving past it? Pretending it didn't happen? Or is this some cruel game, meant to remind me of how wrong we are, how wrong we were and how wrong I am?

He takes his time waiting for Cindy to answer, lifting his beer to his lips. The muscles in his throat move as he takes a long swig, eyes still stuck on hers and I glance up, instinctively searching for my dad, but he's across the room, distracted, laughing with Jack, completely unaware of what's happening. Luckily.

"No… I…" Cindy's voice falters, cracking under his coldness. She's never been able to handle Rook, but he's now something completely different and she knows it.

"It's fine, Cindy," I say softly, forcing a smile her way even as my insides churn.

"Mom," Rook cuts in, his tone sharp, dismissive. "Why don't you go and check on your husband? Let me catch up with Eb."

A cigarette appears between his fingers, shifting his attention away from her, from me, and to the lighter he flicks open. Cindy hesitates, like she's doesn't want to leave us two alone, but eventually, her hands smooth down her red dress nervously as she stands and walks away, leaving us alone for the first time in two long years.

20

For a moment the only sound between us is the faint crackle of tobacco as he takes a deep pull, the smoke curling up his nostrils from his mouth. The sharp scent of smoke coils into the air, swirling between us as he leans back, exhaling.

The pull between us is too much to bear, the air is dense with unspoken anger, unresolved lust, and years of broken promises. My hand trembles slightly as I lean over to the coffee table to my left, gripping the champagne flute, but I hide it well, taking a long sip to steady myself.

Rook doesn't stop watching me, his fingers drumming a slow rhythm against his beer bottle. His movements are calculated. It's a game—one he's always been better at playing, but I won't fold this time. Suddenly, I catch something black moving around his hand on the back of the couch.

Before I can register what it is, he leans forward quickly, the leather of his jacket creaking softly as his elbows rest on his knees, throwing a glance over his shoulder, ensuring no one's paying attention. When his eyes return to mine, they're intense and they drop to my red lips.

"Merry Christmas, Bunny," he murmurs, entirely devoid of the charm that used to make that stupid nickname tolerable, almost lovable. Now, it feels like a weapon, a reminder of everything we used to be, everything we shouldn't have become and my stomach twists.

I hold his stare, refusing to let him see me hesitate, but the nickname pulls at old wounds, opening them just enough to sting. He used to say it because he said Ebony sounded like E-Bunny, and the name stuck, even when it annoyed me. Back then, it meant he loved me like his little sister.

My grip tightens on the glass as I feel the burn of tears threatening to rise. Memories of that Christmas night flash through my mind in vivid, painful detail—how he took my innocence, how he shattered every boundary I thought I had. My breath hitches, and I force myself to push the images down, locking them away where they belong.

"You still remember, don't you?" He asks in a quiet murmur, being discreet around our family, his head tilting to the side. "You can't even fucking look at me without feeling me between your legs, breaking into your virgin pussy."

The vulgarity of his words punches the air from my lungs. I freeze, my blood boiling under my skin as his eyes drag down me again, like he owns the right to look.

"You hate yourself for it, and it's pitiful." He shakes his head slightly, like he's disgusted with me, with everything.

His insult cuts deep, but I refuse to let him have the satisfaction of seeing how much it affects me. Raising my chin, I meet his gaze head-on, narrowing my eyes slightly, daring him to keep pushing.

"Is that really the first thing you want to say to me after two years, Rook?" I scoff and shake my head slightly. "Why am I the pathetic one when you can't stop eye-fucking me in front of our family? What's wrong? Still not moved on from fucking your drunk little sister?"

His eyes blaze, the intensity behind them searing into me. His body tenses from my choice of words, and for a brief second, I think I've gotten under his skin. I lean forward slightly, closing the distance between us just enough to drive my point home.

"You had me," I whisper, the annoyance in my tone sharp. "But you'll never have me like that again. It's time to drop it."

The silence that follows is deafening, a charged current buzzing between us and we stare at one another.

"I've always liked a challenge, Bunny, you know that," he shoots back, his jaw clenching tightly, the grating of his teeth audible before he points at me and my eyes dart downward toward it.

I immediately see a small black snake curling around his tattooed fingers, and I recoil, my throat drying.

"Is… Is that a snake on your hand?"

"You've changed, Bunny," he say's and my eyes flicker upward to his. He searches them, trying to figure out who I am now.

But he's not wrong, I have changed. Life has changed me, shaped me, and I'm not the naive little girl he once knew.

I raise an eyebrow as I answer, "And so have you."

He tilts his head to the side, gaze narrowing as he explores my features. "But what's happened to you?"

My eyes lower, the question hitting me hard. "You would know if you were here," I respond, facing aside.

He pauses, staring at my side-profile for a moment. "And who's fault is that, hm?"

When I glance at him, he doesn't look at me now, drawing away and slumping back on the couch. I can't help but feel the ache in my heart. How we got to this point and everything else. I think back on the very first time I ever felt something shift between us.

It was on a New Year's Eve, and it was the first time I was ever really allowed around Rook and his friends. Me and my friend back then, Taylor, went to a yard party at one of his close friends' houses in hopes to watch a huge fireworks display.

CHAPTER TWO

- FLASHBACK -

As I step out of our home, I flick my black hair over my shoulder before striding down the long pathway. It's late, later than I've ever been out and I spot Rook leaning against his black matte Harley at the end, smoking, looking down at his phone.

I pull my short, white dress further down my thighs, feeling nervous about this party, but I know if Rook's there, I'll be fine.

Approaching I notice his eyes flick upward to me before he double takes. His gaze narrows as he tucks his phone into his pocket, his chin tilting upward before he pushes himself away from the bike, which he names Darkness. When I'm close he shakes his head once, eyes raking down me.

"No. Fucking. Way. In. Hell." He says each word comes through clenched teeth.

25

I roll my eyes, passing him, trying to ignore his stupid brotherly form of possessiveness.

"Fuck off, Rook." I say, ready to get on the back of his bike, but his strong hand around my upper arm stops me, along with his glare.

"I mean it, Bunny." He grits out before giving a head gesture toward the house, "Get your slutty ass back inside and put some pants on."

I yank my arm free and place my hand on my hip. "Excuse me? Did you just call me slutty when you know…"

"Yes. Slut. Get the fuck back inside."

I feel my blood boil and I narrow my eyes. "Say that again, I fucking dare you."

He brings his face close to mine. "Slut." He bites and I raise my hand, ready to smack his smug face, but he catches it before pinning it behind my back, pulling me close.

"Don't fuck with me, Bunny."

"What is wrong with you, psycho!" I yell, struggling in his grasp until he suddenly lets me go.

I stumble back in my heels, fixing myself and when I lift my head, swiping my hair away from my face, I narrow my eyes, pointing my finger.

"You're not my father, Rook. You can't…"

"No, I'm not. I'm worse. I'm your big fucking brother," he cuts me off.

"And it's getting weird." I retort which makes him raise an eyebrow before I continue. "I'm a woman… I'm…"

"You're dressed like a hooker and you're not one," he throws back calmly, flicking his cigarette away and I pause, just staring at him until he closes the gap between us.

"I don't want other guys looking at my little sister like she's some easy piece of meat they can touch. I don't want to have to kill my fucking friends, Eb," he says when he stops right in front of me.

I gaze up at him, getting annoyed with this shit every single time.

"Taylor's brother isn't like this with her."

"Taylor's fucking brother ain't me."

"I figured. You almost sound jealous of the possibility of guys…" I trail off, glancing away but he fingers curl around my chin, tilting my head to look up at him.

He brushes through my hair gently, sweeping it away from my face.

"I do it because I love you, Bunny, that's all," he murmurs, his gaze flickering from my lips to eyes and I feel something flip in my stomach.

It's not unusual for Rook to say that. He's been saying it for years now as siblings, but he's never said it like that—in a way that shoots straight through my soul, while staring at my lips like he wants to…. Fucking kiss me.

He suddenly wraps his arm around the bottom of my back, lifting me effortlessly and before I know it, I'm being dumped on his bike. My heart rate skyrockets as his warm, tatted hands rest on my hips a little too long. We hold eye contact as he gives them a small squeeze then lets me go, a small devilish smirk twitching on his lips.

I just stare at him, confused, until he suddenly grabs the hem of my dress, lifts it and dips down before I can even process what he's doing.

"You better have panties on," he sneers.

I squeal, slamming my thighs together before my leg shoots out, aiming for his balls. But he's too quick and his legs clamp around it, stopping me before his hand shoots up, clutching around my throat. My head snaps back and he hisses aggressively against my lips to warn me.

His fingers dig into my cheeks, pinching tightly and I breath heavily through my nose, my heart thumbing loudly in my ears.

"Red," he grits through tight teeth. "Red silky fucking panties. What is happening to my little Bunny?"

"You like looking at your sisters pussy suddenly?" I shoot back through shallow breaths and squished cheeks.

He snickers, his eyes moving from my lips and eyes repeatedly.

"You shouldn't be doing that," I warn, and he rolls his eyes before refocusing on my gaze.

"I shouldn't be doing this either…" he suddenly leans in to kiss me, but before our lips can collide, we hear the front door of the house open.

Rook releases me in an instant and closes his eyes as he takes a calm step back, allowing me to breathe. As I tilt my head forward, I stare at him with wide eyes, wondering what the fuck is going on with him.

"Don't have her out too long, Rook!" Cindy shouts from the threshold, but we're too locked in eye contact, and I struggle to get air into my lungs.

28

"Yeah, yeah." He answers, his voice as cold as the way he stares at me.

"Happy New Year, you two!" she calls out again before the door slams shut behind her.

"What the fuck was that?" I ask him, but he breaks eye contact, his jaw tense.

Then after a moment, he chuckles and shakes his head. His brows raise as his wipes his hand over his mouth.

"It was just a joke… I'm fucking high," he responds with an unbothered shrug, dropping his hand before dragging his leather jacket down his ripped, tattooed arms, leaving himself in only a tight black tank.

"A joke," I whisper blankly, more to myself.

He takes another step forward, wrapping it over my shoulders and I thread my arms through, the heavy fabric completely drowning my small body. He lifts his helmet and shoves it down on my head before grabbing the front roughly, tilting my head up to look at him.

"If I murder anyone tonight, it's your fault, sis," he warns.

I sigh as I turn my body, and he gets on in front of me. I wrap my arms around his waist, like I always do, but this time everything feels different. Like we've changed. Somethings changed. I can feel deep in my gut, and it scares me. Rook revs the engine before pulling away from the drive.

- PRESENT -

After that night, everything changed between us. Subtly at first, like the smallest crack in a dam, but it didn't stay small for long. He made his move—unexpected, bold, and impossible to ignore. And from there, it was a long, torturous game filled with countless of other moves, each one more calculated and harder to fend off.

I resisted. I fought him, fought myself, fought the growing ache that seemed to seep into every secret glance, every accidental touch, every filthy whispered word. But resisting him was like standing on a path destined to fail.

Everything spiraled out of control from then on. The lines that outlined our relationship—lines we'd both taken for granted—blurred, then disappeared entirely. He stopped pretending to care about the rules, about what was right, and I… I struggled to hold on to what little sense of control I had left. But it wasn't enough. I wanted my brother. I wanted him so fucking badly.

Our relationship took dangerous, forbidden turns, the kind that left me lying awake at night, wrestling with guilt and desire. I tried to shove the pieces of us back into something that resembled normalcy and our family, but Rook didn't back down. He never did. He pushed harder and firm, breaking me down bit by bit.

Until that Christmas one year later, when everything I'd tried so desperately to hold together finally unraveled.

CHAPTER THREE

As I stare at Ebony from across from me, my little pet snake, Ouija, slithering slothfully around my hand. Her smooth black scales glide through my fingers, a calming distraction from the madness of my thoughts. But even as she winds herself into knots, my focus is locked on Bunny.

My beautiful little sister.

Too beautiful for her own fucking good. For my good.

Being here was a mistake. A massive fucking mistake. Two years of forced banishment should have been enough. Enough time to forget the way she feels under my skin. How she smells. Enough time to carve out the part of me that still craves her, despite everything. But I hadn't stayed away because I didn't want to see her—God, I wanted to see her. No, I stayed away because the last time we were together, she made it painfully clear where I stood.

She wasn't willing to fight for me the way I wanted to fight for her. She didn't want us the way I did. She shattered me that Christmas, every fucking piece of my heart breaking apart and leaving nothing behind but a hollow, black void in its place.

Still, distance didn't keep me from her completely. Nothing could. She was a siren call, a compulsion I couldn't shake, a sickness I didn't want cured. I watched her every chance I got. Hacked her computers, her phones, every goddamn camera she owned. I watched her when she didn't know I was there—every moment stolen through a lens.

I saw her undress, her skin glowing in the dim light of her room. I watched her touch herself, her heavy, blue eyes glued to whatever pitiful porn she thought could satisfy her. I read every pathetic message she sent and received. Listened to her pointless conversations.

And every single time, it drove me closer to the edge. How many nights did I sit on my bike, ready to ride here and kidnap her? Too fucking many to count. Too many nights spent staring into the darkness of what we could never have and wanting it anyway. Then Blaise happened three months ago.

She didn't choose him. That was obvious. Her dad made sure of it, forcing her into some half-assed arrangement with that worthless fucker. But it was then that I made the choice to stop. To stop watching, stop waiting, stop torturing myself with every glimpse of her life without me. It was killing me—slowly, fucking heartbreakingly.

Not being near her was one thing, a pain I'd almost grown used to. But when I started to have to watch her with him—that was unbearable. Every kiss he stole, every touch he dared to lay on her that wasn't mine, it made me want to ride off a cliff.

But the truth is, none of it dulled the itch inside me. The one only she can scratch. The one that digs deeper every time I try to ignore it. Every time I tell myself this is wrong. She's like a fire burning through me, and no matter how much it hurts, I can't put it out. Ebony isn't just my sister. She's my goddamn soulmate. She always has been. She always fucking will be.

And that's what makes it insufferable. Knowing she's mine in every way that matters—except the only way I want her to be.

I watch as she shrugs off her fur jacket, the soft material sliding down her bronzed, sun-kissed skin, which gleams with a golden shimmer under the glow of the Christmas lights. I notice she's finally got ink, which surprises me. A full sleeve painted up her right arm and it only makes her even more perfect.

Her glittery black dress clings to her curves, sculpted to her body like it was made for her, the neckline plunging low enough to reveal the swell of her big tits.

She's always had those—melons—round, full, fucking impossible to ignore—but now, she's more than just the girl I knew. She's grown into herself in ways that make it difficult for me to look away.

Her hips are fuller now, her body softer in all the right places, and I can't stop myself from taking in every small detail. She's not just beautiful. She's the kind of breathtaking that makes my chest tighten and my dick hard. Every inch of her radiates the confidence and sexuality of a woman who doesn't realize just how intoxicating she is. She's never seen herself the way I do. Always the introvert, the quiet one, shrinking back into the shadows like she doesn't belong in the spotlight. In her mind, there's always someone better—prettier, smarter, louder. Someone more deserving. But not to me. To me, she's fucking flawless.

33

But speaking to her now, it's clear—she's not the same girl I left behind. I see it in her eyes, that harsh glint. I hear it in her voice, the strictness. It's the same tone she used the last time I saw her, the one that gutted me when she gave up on me.

She doesn't take bullshit anymore. Life has hardened and reshaped her into someone who stands taller and speaks louder. And I can't help but wonder if losing me did this to her, the same way losing her crushed and rebuilt me into something darker, something angrier.

Maybe she's been walking through her own kind of silent hell, just like me. And maybe, just maybe, that's why she looks so damn untouchable now—like she's wearing her pain as armor. But that only makes me want to touch her more. To put her in her place and destroy her in the process. It's a twisted need I've had for so many years, and it seems it hasn't stopped. I want to dominate her all over again, to take her beneath me and remind her who she belongs to, make her surrender.

I think back to the years that molded us—the time that warped everything into what it is now. When I first met Ebony, I was twelve, and she was ten. I hated her on sight. She was the daughter of the man I despised with every ounce of my being. Ryker—the motherfucker who tore my father's club to pieces and pissed on its fucking ashes the second he got the chance. The man my father loathed until his dying breath. And then, as if the universe wanted to spit in my face, I was forced to live under Ryker's roof.

I avoided her at first. She was just another piece of his legacy, a reminder of everything I'd lost. But the years had their way of changing things. Ebony went from an annoyance to the only thing keeping me sane. She became my world without me even realizing it. I loved her. Not like I loved my mom or anyone else.

No, it was a fierce, consuming kind of love. I protected her at all costs, maybe aggressively so. But then, everything started to change.

By the time we hit our late teens, that love—brotherly love, I had—morphed into something dark and obsessive. I was jealous. Every guy who looked at her, every friend she made, every moment she spent away from me—it burned me up inside. I found myself watching her when she didn't know. Thinking about her riding my cock, her titties bouncing, when I should've been doing something else.

Even in the kitchen in the mornings as she ate her cereal, half asleep, no make-up, hair like she has been yanked through a fucking bush backward, I wanted nothing more than to bend her over the table and ram my cock inside her. It wasn't enough to be near her anymore; I wanted to possess her completely.

Then, finally, I wanted to ruin her for anyone else. To touch her, claim her, make her understand she was only ever meant to belong to me. The idea of taking her innocence—making her mine in a way no one could undo—consumed me. It was forbidden, dangerous, and utterly fucking mind-altering.

So, I started testing the waters. Made small moves. Pushing boundaries. Showing her, in ways I hoped only she'd notice, that I didn't see her just as my little sister anymore. That she was something so much more.

I knew the risks. Knew Ryker would kill me in a heartbeat if he ever found out. But I didn't give a flying fuck. I would've died for her then, and I still would now. Because in my dark, broken world, Ebony wasn't just everything to me—she was me. And there was no way I was letting anyone else take her before I do.

That Christmas night in the cabin wasn't just a mistake or a moment of weakness—it was fate. I've played it over in my mind a thousand times, and no matter how much she might hate me for it now, I know the truth. She loved it. Every filthy second of it. The way her body responded to me, the way she surrendered. The way we collided that night was everything I had fantasized about.

She wasn't just the girl I thought I knew; she was so much more. She gave herself to me in a way that made everything—every risk, every fucking consequence—worth it. She was everything I knew she would be. She consumed me that Christmas, just like I fucking consumed her. I lost it that night.

And no matter how much time has passed, I haven't stopped thinking about it. About her. About the way she tasted, the way she sounded, the way she felt around me. That night was the point of no return. It wasn't just a moment—it was a reckoning. One I'm not sure either of us can ever escape.

CHAPTER FOUR

- THAT CHRISTMAS TWO YEARS AGO -

ROOK

In Ryker's sprawling lake house cabin, I sit perched on a barstool in the kitchen, cradling another beer like it's the only thing chaining me to this place. The whole family is here, like they are every fucking Christmas Eve, but this year, Ryker's added a few outsiders—friends of the family, guests that crowd the space and suffocate the air. The festive chaos grates on my sanity, so I've tucked myself away in this corner.

As I tilt the bottle back, eyes fixed on the ceiling for a moment, they instinctively fall back to her. Through the double doors that lead to the living room, I watch Bunny. She moves in time with the Christmas music blasting through the house, snow falling heavily outside the frosted windows. The twinkling Christmas lights cast her in a golden haze, their cheer mocking my dreary mood.

Her short red dress hugs her in all the right places, the neckline dipping low. A dress I would usually kill her for, but luckily, she's here, with family. A pair of ridiculous reindeer antlers sits atop her head, making her look even more infuriatingly adorable. She's laughing, carefree, with Tiffany, her cousin who's about the same age. The two of them sway together, Tiffany's arm looping through hers as they spin, drawing the attention of nearly every guy in the room.

I grip the beer bottle harder, my knuckles whitening as I slam it down on the counter. She's always been oblivious to the way she pulls focus; how every goddamn movement she makes commands attention. Or maybe she isn't oblivious at all. Maybe she just doesn't give a fuck about us anymore. My chest tightens at the thought, a bitter swell of selfishness crawling up my throat.

I should look away, but I can't. She's the only thing I can see, the only thing I've ever really seen in this house full of people I couldn't give less of a shit about. Every laugh, every smile digs deeper into me. I want her so fucking bad. She's trying to avoid me at the moment. Trying to stay away from me because shit's getting heated between us and it's driving me crazy.

I glance up at the clock hanging on the wall, its ticking blurred by the fog of too many beers. Midnight is creeping closer, the threshold to Christmas almost here. My gaze drifts back toward her—Ebony. And then I see him. A guy I barely know stepping into her orbit, talking to her. My drunken haze clears instantly, my focus sharpening as if my body's instinct is to fight.

She laughs at something he says, and my jaw tightens so hard it's a miracle my teeth don't crack. Then, as if she can feel my gaze burning into her, she hesitantly looks over her shoulder. Our eyes collide—hers unfocused from the alcohol, mine hard and cutting through the distance between us. A warning.

Her expression shifts, her carefree attitude replaced by something else entirely. Guilt? Fear? Whatever it is, she knows the rules. She knows what happens when another guy tries to step where he doesn't belong. What the fuck am I supposed to do? Sit back and let someone else fucking touch her? Over my dead body. If I have to live with this torture, then so does she. She's mine, whether she wants to admit it or not.

I see it in her face—reluctance, a moment where she considers the backlash. But then disobedience sparks in her eyes. She tucks her bottom lip between her teeth, and I can see her thinking.

Don't fucking do it.

And then she does. Bold as hell, or maybe just too drunk to care, she turns and walks off with him, out of my sight.

The instant they disappear, something snaps. My fist slams down on the wooden counter, the sound echoing through the cheery kitchen. I shove the stool back with a scrape and round the island, ignoring the glances from anyone nearby.

I stalk toward the living room, shoving past groups of family and friends, their laughter and music scratching against my ears like nails on a chalkboard. I don't care about the festivities, the people, or the goddamn snow falling outside. There's only one thought on my mind, and it's her.

I search every room, frustration mounting with every step, but Ebony seems to have disappeared into thin air. When I've scoured every corner, I head to the back door, the cold air hitting my hot skin as I step outside. My breath clouds in the night air, and the sound of voices catches my attention—soft and low, coming from around the side of the house.

The snow crunches under my boots as I move, my pulse hammering in my ears and when I turn the corner, I see them.

39

She's leaning back against the wooden siding, her figure illuminated by the faint glow of the Christmas lights reflecting off the heavy snowfall. And that guy, the one who clearly doesn't know who the fuck I am or what I'm capable of—has his arm braced above her head, his body angled toward hers, trapping her. My teeth grind as I take in the scene as she places her hand on his chest, shaking her head once, saying something I can't hear, but it doesn't fucking matter.

I don't waste a second. My boots dig into the snow as I stride toward them, the sound of my approach loud. The guy's head snaps toward me first, his face painted with confusion, but it's her reaction that cuts me to the bone. Her eyes widen, panic flashing across her face like she's been caught in the act. She pushes against his chest quickly, a move that looks desperate, as if it will somehow change what I just saw.

It doesn't.

My fists clench at my sides, and I close the distance, my body thrumming with barely contained rage.

"Rook—" Ebony starts, but I don't even stop to think.

Without hesitation, I swing my fist hard, the crack of bone meeting bone echoing in the freezing air. The uppercut lifts him clean off his feet before he crashes onto the snow with a heavy thud.

"Rook!" Ebony's scream cuts through the manic, but my focus is too locked on the guy groaning at my feet.

His pathetic attempts to roll away only fuel the fire inside me. I kick him in the stomach, once, twice, each strike harder than the last, knocking the air out of him as he writhes in the snow. My mind blanks out her frantic cries and her tugging at my leather jacket. All I can hear is the pounding of blood in my ears and the sickening satisfaction of his gasps for breath.

I lean down, grabbing his throat, my fingers tightening like a vice. His eyes bulge, his hands clawing weakly at mine as I squeeze, my grip unrelenting. "Touch her again, and I'll fucking kill you," I growl, though I'm not even sure if the words leave my mouth. The murderous red haze has completely taken over.

Suddenly, a tight grip on my jacket yanks me backward with a force that only one man could muster—Ryker.

I stumble back, the cold rushing in as his hold releases. Breathing heavily, I straighten, glaring at him. He stands between me and the gasping guy on the ground, his face unreadable, his calm an eerie opposite to the rage inside me. My angry gaze flicks to Ebony, her wide eyes brimming with tears.

I grunt, straightening my jacket with a rough pull, and without another word, I turn, storming back inside the house, leaving the chaos and the bitter cold behind me.

Ebony

In the kitchen, the hushed chatter of leaving guests fades as the mansion begins to empty. The silence that follows the sudden cutoff of Christmas music feels like a vacuum, pulling me into the dark corners of my thoughts. I lower my head into my hands, my elbows resting on the cool countertop, and exhale shakily.

Rook's face flashes in my mind—the fury etched into every line, the fire blazing in his eyes as he looked at me. I went too far this time. Pushing him was a mistake, one that almost cost that guy his life. But as guilt gnaws at me, another thought surfaces, darker and angrier: When will this end?

He can't keep doing this. He can't keep controlling everything I do. This thing between us—it's toxic. It's dangerous. And it's gonna destroy us both. I've felt it creeping closer and my dad isn't blind to what's happening. He's not a stupid man. Every day, his gaze lingers a little too long, his questions cut a little too deep. He knows something's wrong. He sees the difference between Rook's natural protectiveness and the possessiveness that now radiates from him like a warning sign.

And Rook? He doesn't give a shit. He's reckless in a way that terrifies me, willing to risk it all—his life, my life—just to keep this twisted connection alive between us. It's not love anymore. It's desperation, an unhinged obsession that threatens to wreck everything in its path.

I press my palms harder against my temples, as if I can somehow block it out in my mind. My heart aches, torn between what I know is right and the gravitational pull that Rook has always had on me.

How do I stop him? How do I stop myself?

When I hear footsteps behind me, I lift my head, still feeling the haze from the alcohol in my system. My father enters and moves across the kitchen before pouring himself a whiskey at the far end of the island. I avoid looking at him, keeping my gaze fixed on the countertop.

The space between us feels charged, especially now when all I want to do is think about Rook, the mess we've created, and the anger and confusion I can't seem to stop. But where did he go after everything? I haven't seen him since the fight outside, and him not being here feels like a wound I can't stop picking at.

I hear my father knock back the whiskey with a hiss, the sound of the glass slamming back onto the counter making me jump, my body reacting involuntarily. I squirm in my seat as he rounds the island, his heavy footsteps drawing closer. I can feel his gaze on me even before I dare lift my eyes.

When he finally reaches me, he leans both his forearms on the counter, his face coming close. My stomach tightens, and I stare into his blue eyes, trying to hold my ground. The intensity of his gaze is a force, like he's searching for something I'm not willing to give.

"Everything okay, princess?" he asks, his voice taking on a fatherly softness that always makes my insides coil uncomfortably.

I don't know why but hearing him say that makes something inside me want to break. I want to scream that it's not okay, that everything inside me feels like it's falling apart, but I don't. Instead, I stay quiet, a lump forming in my throat.

Sometimes, just sometimes, I wonder if I could tell him. If I could say the words and explain how Rook and I—how we can't

43

seem to escape each other. But then I think of how my father would react. I imagine his face, the fury and disgust that would settle in his eyes. He'd never accept it. He sees Rook as a threat, as much as Rook sees him the same. And me? His daughter, his baby girl—he would never allow us to cross that line. To him, Rook and I are strangely family. End of story.

He watches me, studying me so closely, as if he can see right through my skin. I've always hated how well he knows me—how he can tell when I'm hiding something. He's Ryker Huxley, after all. Known for sniffing out weakness, for tearing down every wall you think you've built. There's no fooling him. Not for long.

I swallow, feeling the lie before it even leaves my lips. He doesn't say anything, but I can feel his eyes lowering, watching the way my throat constricts.

To get him off my back, I force a soft smile, one that's phony, and shake my head. "I'm fine, Daddy," I say nervously. "I think I'm just tired. It's been a long night."

The smile doesn't reach my eyes. I can see the hesitation in his, but he doesn't press further. Not yet. He simply nods, lingering before he leans over, pressing his lips against my forehead.

"Merry Christmas, Ebony. Go get some shut eye and I'll see you in the morning."

Noel of Sin

I stagger down the shadowy upstairs corridor, each step heavy, my mind blurred from the drink. The bathroom door looms ahead like a dark portal. I shove it open, my hands shaking as I flick the light on, flooding the room with harsh brightness. I slam the door shut behind me and kick off my shoes, my body yearning for sleep. The mirror calls me, pulling my gaze. I'm a mess. Smudged mascara streaks down my face, the result of a night gone too far.

I twist the faucet open and scoop water into my hands, splashing myself with cold water. The shock of it stings, but it doesn't numb the gnawing feeling inside me. I rub my face, trying to scrub away the evidence of a night I can't control. When the make-up is gone, I fumble behind me, unclipping my bra and tossing it aside, letting my heavy breasts fall freely in my red dress. I yawn, the room spinning as I flick off the light and step back into the hallway.

The dimness of a distant light from downstairs at the end of the hall is my only guide. My hand skims the walls, searching for the cool metal of a doorknob. I don't care which room I end up in. It doesn't matter. There's so many rooms in this damn Lakehouse. I twist one, the door creaking open and I barely notice the soft glow of Christmas lights tangled around a headboard as I shut the door behind me.

As I move toward the bed, another yawn escapes me, but this time, longer, louder and my eyes scrunch closed. My knees hit the mattress, and I yank the covers back, crawling under before wrapping them tightly around me. But just as I feel I'm about to drift into a deep slumber, something moves behind me.

My eyes snap open, wide, but before I can react, a powerful arm wraps around my waist, dragging me back forcefully against a solid, bare chest. The suffocating weight of a hand presses over my mouth, muffling my breath. Every muscles tenses, my heart hammering in my chest, adrenaline flooding my veins. Rook lifts his head, looking down at my panicked side-profile. Fuck. I'm in his bed by accident.

"Well, well, well. Aren't you a silly Christmas bunny." His low growl vibrates against my ear, a warning laced with desire.

His hand suddenly moves down the front of my body and I freeze, but only for a second. His fingers sneak beneath the fabric of my panties, pushing in with a force that makes my stomach flip. My hand shoots out, gripping his thick wrist to stop him, but not enough to truly fight him off. His fingers press harder, through my lips, finding my clit and a shudder runs through my thighs, my body betraying me as a soft moan slips against his hand.

His intentions are clear. He has me now, alone. In his bed. And nothing's going to stop him. He's finally not taking any more of my resistance.

He pulls his hand out of panties, only to yank my thigh open, exposing me completely, a silent, dominant demand to keep them wide. My breath catches as I meet his dark, predatory gaze, and he slips his hand back inside, his fingers exploring me with a brutality that makes my chest tighten and my pussy throb.

He moves with purpose, no hesitation, no tenderness. Every inch of me is claimed, touched, violated, from front to back—nothing left untouched, nothing left for me to hide.

"See, you're always waiting—wondering when I'll drag you to the edge again, when I'll force it on you so you can surrender because we both know you'll fall. You want to drown in sin, don't you, little sister? In me and this twisted fucking hunger we're not supposed to feed but can't seem to starve."

He's not wrong, I can feel it in the roughness of his touch, it ignites something inside me. It floods me, needy and desperate, a wave of arousal and humiliation crashing over me in waves. I can feel myself, shamefully far too wet and eager already, but he doesn't care. He smears my come, spreads it over me, relishing how soaked he's making me.

Forbidden, warped desire rips through me, my innocence gradually being pulled from the inside out. This is wrong. So, fucking wrong. This is my big brother. But my body—my traitorous body—burns with the heat of it. It feels like everything I've ever wanted, even if I can't admit it. This is why I've tried to avoid him lately. The anger, the hatred, the way he makes me feel so powerless. I can't stand him sometimes, and yet, here I am. Allowing it.

The moment he realizes I'm enjoying it, my hips bucking instinctively against his hand, begging for more, he removes the one clamped over my mouth. I gasp, desperate to find my voice on instinct, to stop what feels inevitable.

"We can't—" I whisper, but he's already on me, his breath hot and sharp as his snarl cuts through the air between us.

"Shut the fuck up before our parents kill us both. You think you can flirt with other guys? Your little cunt is desperate for it, but it will only ever be for me. It always has been and tonight, my bunny, I'm breaking you the fuck in."

The words snap through me but before I can even draw another breath, his lips crash against mine. The kiss is bruising, desperate, his tongue invading my mouth with a feral hunger. His dominance is too much, and I'm left struggling to keep up. My inexperience is a stark contrast to his, but his intensity and our connection pulls me under, sweeping me away with every flick of his tongue.

47

And then there's his hand. His fingers tease and torment, stroking my swollen clit with a devastating accuracy. Each movement sends fire rippling through me, my body betraying me as it arches, shivers, yields.

Just as I start to really get into it, he pulls back suddenly, leaving my lips swollen and tingling. My protest dies in my throat as his hand slaps over my mouth again, silencing me. His green gaze is piercing, dark and heavy, holding me captive as his fingers slide lower.

My heart pounds, my entire body taut as he presses against my wet entrance, taking a small pause, like he might be hesitating himself, but then, he pushes past it and starts to slip a finger inside my untouched pussy. I realize I've already surrendered, whether I wanted to or not and my eyes close, the sensation of the small stretch evading my senses.

I hold my breath as he pushes deeper, his finger sinking in until it's buried to the knuckle. The pressure leaves every nerve ending alight and his finger doesn't stop; he starts to slip it in and out, slow and steady, teasing me.

I can feel him watching me, his gaze heavy, like he's unraveling me with his eyes. Each stroke against my walls pulls a small sound from my throat, a broken whimper I can't contain.

"Shhh…" he breathes against the shell of my ear softly. "If you want me to keep touching your little virgin pussy, you're going to have to be so fucking quiet for me, Eb."

I nod without meaning to, a silent agreement, my body already betraying my mind. His finger continues dragging against my walls in a way that leaves me gasping into his palm.

"Good girl," he murmurs, his voice dark and approving as I shudder beneath him.

He removes his hand from my mouth gently, almost teasingly, letting my muffled breaths escape into the air. His lips linger above mine, so close they almost brush, but instead of kissing me, he slides his finger out again. This time, another one nudges against my hole, testing the limits of what I can take.

My body clenches in protest as he pushes them in, a sharp gasp escaping as the pressure builds. He doesn't stop. His fingers force me open, inch by inch, in a way that feels unbearable and consuming all at once. He reads every flicker of pain, every shiver of conflict. He takes it all in, as if he's searing every moment in his mind forever.

My thighs tremble as I struggle to adjust, and when he finally sinks to the base of his knuckles, a low growl rumbles from deep in his chest.

His gaze flicks to my lips, lingering there, but I know Rook. I know what he wants, what he's always wanted. To ruin me. He's said it enough times, and the sinister glint in his eyes tells me that it's taking everything inside him not to finger bang me right away.

When he draws his fingers back, the friction makes me gasp, and he closes his eyes, exhaling like he's cherishing every second of it. His forehead presses against mine, and for a brief moment, it almost feels gentle. Almost. Then, without warning, he shoves them back inside me.

The force knocks the breath from my lungs, a silent scream catching in my throat as pain blossoms between my legs. My thighs snap shut around his hand, my body shuddering as the sting crashes over me.

His eyes flash open, locking onto mine with a fierce, almost punishing intensity. "Fucking spread them," he snarls quietly. "You're gonna take what I do to you."

I meet his gaze, a small silent plea, but he shakes his head in return, his forehead still pressed against mine.

"You should know better than that, Bunny," he murmurs. "This? This is nothing. I'm breaking you in slowly for your sake, because I love you. But when I'm balls deep inside this perfect pussy, I'm tearing you the fuck apart. Piece by fucking piece."

My chest heaves, thighs shaking as I try to process what he's just said, but the truth is, I already know. Whether through pain or pleasure, it didn't matter—he was always going to make sure I'd never stop feeling it. Never stop feeling us.

"Take off your panties," he orders, and I lower my hands to my hips, taking the strings before easing them down my legs.

With his fingers still sunk deep inside me, he shifts, rising sinuously, his movements careful as he positions himself between my legs. My eyes trail down his incredible body, taking in the ink that marks his skin, every muscle that flexes against the twinkling Christmas fairy lights above us.

He leans over me, forearm planted beside my head on the pillow and his mouth hovers achingly close to mine. Slowly, he slides his fingers out of me and my breath catches as I feel him smear a slick mixture of my come—and possibly blood—across my tender, throbbing pussy.

Before I can even process the humiliation or heat of it, his fingers sink back inside me, then he starts to fuck me with them. The rhythm is steady, each thrust a perfect balance of pain and promise. My eyes squeeze shut, my body writhing beneath him as I chase the flickers of pleasure.

50

His hand finds its way behind my head, tangling in my hair before yanking it back hard, asserting his control over me. A whimper escapes as the tension forces my neck to arch, exposing my throat to him. Vulnerable. Open. Exactly how he wants me.

He dips his head, his tongue and teeth working in perfect unison, attacking my neck with a brutal kind of seductiveness. He sucks and bites, branding me with every mark he lays on my skin. Each nip stings and soothes all at once and it has my head spinning. His legs remain firmly between mine, pinning me open, forcing me to endure everything he's giving me without escape.

His fingers grow more ruthless, hitting deeper, rougher, and my body surrenders completely. The wetter I get, the more determined he becomes, the curve of his fingers destructive. When he starts to curl them just right, hitting something inside me that makes my vision blur, I start hyperventilating. It's a sensation I've never felt before, it's different to the other times I've experienced oral orgasms by him, and it pulls a strangled, shameful moan from deep in my throat that I can barely stifle.

Every nerve in my body is alive, tingling, as something builds inside me with startling intensity. The wave rises fast, impossibly fast, just like my breathing. I ride the peak, every hard thrust of his fingers sending me higher, until finally, it crashes over me.

The release tears through me like a lightning strike, white-hot and all-consuming. My muscles jerk uncontrollably as my pussy tightens and pulses around his fingers. The pleasure is too much, too quick, yet impossibly perfect, and I can't stop myself from falling apart beneath him.

But he doesn't stop.

His fingers continue their ruthless plunges, drawing the aftershocks out into a searing, unbearable high. My body feels helpless against the way he's wringing me out, heightening the sensation.

Finally, he calms his movements and lifts his head, his lips inches from mine as the remnants of what he's just unleashed, gradually fading. As my hips twitch against his hand, bucking against it, his gaze is dark, pupils blown, burning with something almost feral, but his mouth is gentle as he brushes it over mine, kissing me softly.

I'm breathless, undone, my mind spiraling from the haze of pleasure but one thought pierces through the fog.

I need more. I need him. All. Of. Him.

My hand glides up the length of his arm, the tension beneath his skin thrumming against my fingertips, until I'm wrapping it around his broad shoulders. My fingers find their way into the thick strands of his dark hair, threading through and tugging lightly as I catch myself. My other hand moves, trailing down the front of his body, grazing over the ridges of his hard abs.

Our eyes stay locked, a silent war of control and surrender, as my fingers dip beneath the waistband of his boxers. The heat radiates against my palm as I slip inside, the rough texture of his pubic hair brushing against my skin, guiding me to where I need to be.

I find him, my hand wrapping around his cock, and my breath halts. He's too thick, too long, the heaviness of him in my hand enough to make me clench my thighs together and run. His lips part slightly, a breath hissing out as my grip tightens. I drag my palm downward, feeling every ridge, every bulging vein, every detail of his rock-hard dick beneath my fingers.

His eyes grow darker, a storm brewing in them as a low, guttural growl escapes his throat. My thumb brushes over the slick tip, the cool metal of the piercing that I've always known was there, gliding over the pad, and I bite my lip to stifle a whimper, feeling the need pouring into me like a greedy wave.

"Are you going to fuck me now, Rook?" I whisper, my voice breathless, yet daring. "Are you going to take my virginity and make me yours like you've always promised?"

The words linger in the air, and I know I've lit a fire that neither of us is prepared to put out. This is my surrender to him. Finally. I'm giving into what we both want. What we both need. Right now, the consequence doesn't matter enough for me to stop.

He doesn't respond, he withdraws his fingers from me, the slick drag making me tremor with the sudden emptiness. For a moment, I think he'll leave me hanging in this deprived state, but then he lifts his hand to his mouth. His gaze locks with mine as he sucks on his fingers, tasting me, and the wet sound fills the space between us before he spits on the tips.

I free his cock from his boxers, hefty in my hand. The heat of him pulses against my palm as I drag my fingers down the length, admiring but fearful of the sheer size of him. He grabs it from me, smearing the spit over the tip.

Before I can catch my breath, his hands grip my hips, yanking me further beneath him and the force of it sends a thrill shooting through me, my body falling completely under his control.

With one swift motion, he gathers the fabric of my red dress in his fists, pulling it up my body. The friction against my skin is quick and he doesn't stop until the dress is over my head, leaving me utterly naked.

As soon as my breasts bounce free, his hungry eyes take me in briefly, and I don't even feel shy about being naked in front of my big brother. That's weird, isn't it? That's got to be weird.

Then he's on me, his large body presses down on mine, the searing heat of him engulfing me, and the skin-to-skin contact makes my nipples hard in an instant. His lips find mine with a kiss that's desperate, as if he's starving for me, and I kiss him back with the same urgency, no longer hesitant, no longer holding back.

It's wet, it's fucking messy, but it's us. The way we move together feels so effortless, so right, like our bodies were made to fit this way.

He dips his hips, pressing his big cock against my wet pussy, teasing me, rubbing it along my slit. I gasp into his mouth, unable to stop myself from wanting more, my arms tightening around his shoulders, clinging myself to him.

His teeth bite into my bottom lip, sucking with a tug before his tongue thrusts down my throat again, claiming me with a savage hunger. Every touch, every kiss, seems to connect us in a way I don't want to escape.

Then, without no more hesitation, he presses the tip of his pierced cock against my entrance. The sharp pain that follows as he pushes forward is almost too much, and I have to break the kiss, straining for air.

My body arches beneath him, instinctively trying to adjust to the burn of him filling and stretching me. He presses his face into the crook of my neck, his breath ragged as he whispers darkly, "You might want to bite down, bunny. This won't be fucking easy at first. Relax and let me take control."

I do as he tells me, sinking my teeth into his shoulder and he hisses. I attempt to relax, to let him press deeper, but it hurts. He feels massive inside me and my legs tense instinctively, my body fighting against the intrusion, but he doesn't falter. He continues, pushing further, ripping through every barrier I have until finally, he's fully inside me.

A shuddered breath escapes me, mirrored by his, as we both pause. His chest heaves against mine as we take in what just happened. Slowly, his head lifts, his heavy eyes meeting mine. My gaze softens, and our connection solidifies, a silent understanding passing between us.

His lips curve before his expression darkens again. His gaze falls to my mouth, lingering for a beat, and then he's on them. His mouth claims mine in a kiss so intense it steals my breath. His tongue sweeps over mine, dominating, demanding, and I surrender.

As his hips flex, he pulls back, gliding his cock along my walls, then he thrusts back in, slow at first, but I whimper into the kiss, my nails biting into his shoulders as his pace begins to quicken. He groans low in his throat, the sound rough and raw, and I fucking love the sound of it.

With every drive inside me, my body gives way to him, the pain melting into a pleasure so intense it leaves me reeling. My walls tighten around him, the slick heat between us making each stroke smoother, deeper. I lose myself in the rhythm he sets, the way his cock fills me over and over again, erasing the chains of our world away until there's nothing left but us.

When he realizes I'm taking him easier, I can feel the change in him, the last threads of his control snapping. The dominance radiates off him, tangible and electric. He tears his lips from mine, and before I can process what's happening, his strong hands snatch my wrists. His thrusts ease, never stopping, but his focus sharpens. I'm so lost in the haze of lust that I barely register the cool, rough press of Christmas lights being wound tightly around my wrists. The cords bite into my skin as he secures me to the headboard, locking me into place.

His breathing grows heavier, rough with barely contained frustration, as he pulls more of the lights. The tension in the room thickens as I feel him loop one behind my knee, yanking it high and wide until it's pressed beside my shoulder. The vulnerability of my position sending a wave of both terror and arousal coursing through me. He does the same to my other leg, restraining and positioning me so I'm spread wide open for him, utterly at his mercy.

His hand glides up the center of my body, his palm leaving a trail of heat in its wake. It doesn't stop until it wraps around my throat, his grip firm, possessive. He leans in close, his lips ghosting just a breath away from mine, and the darkness in his green eyes sends a shiver down my spine.

"I'm going to fuck you exactly how I want to fuck you now, little sister," he snarls, low and menacing. "Your tight cunt is mine to destroy, to break in fully, and you're going to take it. Every agonizing, pleasurable second of it. You're going to come for me again and again, until we're both red and raw from the friction. I don't stop until I think it's enough. Do you understand?"

I swallow against his hand, searching his eyes before giving a small nod, mentally preparing myself for the onslaught I'm about to feel.

"Words, Bunny. Use your fucking words. Tell me." He whispers forcefully, his hand tightening on my neck.

My teeth sink into my bottom lip, and for a moment, I hesitate, feeling ashamed of what I'm about to admit. But we're already passed it. We've already crossed the big red line.

"Fuck me hard, big brother," I whisper, my tone cracking but sure. "Show me how much you've wanted this. How much you've wanted me. Make me never forget it."

A growl tears from his throat as he slaps his hand over my mouth, silencing me with firm pressure. His other hand grips the headboard, knuckles white as he holds it steady, anchoring us both. At first, his thrusts are steady, making me feel every inch of him. But it doesn't last.

Soon, he's slamming into me, his cock driving so deep it feels like he's touching places no one ever could—like I can feel him in my fucking stomach. My legs tense, my body trembling uncontrollably, and the screams I can't hold back are muffled against his hand. The relentless force of him, the overwhelming sensations, consume me entirely.

He makes me come,

Once,

Twice,

Three times—

I've lost fucking count, the pleasure shattering me over and over.

I'm dripping, I can feel the mattress beneath me is soaked with my come and blood, my thighs slick, and his drenched cock glides in and out with a wet, filthy sound that fills the room. He doesn't even slow down, as if the mess we've made only drives him more savage.

His hips slap against my skin with power, echoing through the room and my legs strain against the Christmas lights, the bindings digging into my flesh as his pace becomes brutal. A fleeting thought flickers in the back of my mind—what if someone hears us? But it's drowned out by the sweeping sensation of him.

I always knew Rook was insane. But this? He's lost himself, his mind crazed by me, by this. He's not just fucking me—he's rewriting me, violating me for anyone else. With every thrust, he carves himself into me, so deeply, so thoroughly, that I know I'll never be the same. My innocence is long gone now, it's been torn right out me by my big brother. And I crave it. I want him to destroy me, to let his darkness seep into me, winding itself around my soul.

When he comes the first time, he pulls out quickly, his cock twitching as warm ropes of his jizz pump over my swollen, battered pussy as he jerks himself off. The heat of it soothes the throbbing for a stolen second. His forehead presses against mine, his breath coming in heavy bursts as we cling to the wreckage we just created.

The room is thick with the scent of our sweat and sex, and I can barely breathe, each inhale shallow as I struggle to recover. But the respite is short-lived. I see it—a flicker in his eyes, dark and unreadable. Before I can process it, he grabs his hard cock again and plunges back into me in one swift, devastating stroke. A cry tears from my throat, muffled by his hand, the mix of pain and pleasure overpowering.

He doesn't hold back. He fucks me violently, my tits bouncing wildly. I sense the pent-up frustration pouring out of him with every thrust. It's all there—the hunger, the longing, and something deeper, riskier. Love. Distorted, uncontrollable, undeniable love.

Suddenly, he removes his hand from my mouth, and before I can catch my breath, his lips crush mine in a feral kiss. It's desperate and full of everything he can't say. My body tenses beneath him as his hips drive into me, but then his hands move, both gripping the sparkling headboard for leverage.

My legs hang limply in the Christmas lights now, twitching and numb, utterly dead from his harsh speed. And then, just as I'm about to come undone again, his rhythm changes. His thrusts become more controlled, as his mouth moves against mine with tenderness.

The kiss softens, his lips brushing mine in a way that steals my breath all over again. A low moan escapes me, spilling into his mouth as his cock fills me so completely, so perfectly, I can't imagine ever wanting anything else.

"That's my good little sister. Look at you—you're taking my cock so well. You were always made for me, for this devastation. You were born to be my beautifully, ruined obsession," he whispers breathlessly against my mouth.

He trails kisses down the line of my jaw, and I tilt my head back with a gasp, the sensation making my skin shiver.

"I'm going to fill this sweet little pussy with my cum now," he whispers against the shell of my ear.

His mouth then claims my nipple, biting and sucking, pulling moans from my throat that I can't control. Both his hands find my throat, squeezing as he presses down, pushing me deeper into the pillow, his eyes glittering with sinful darkness.

I gasp, desperate for air, but he doesn't care. He doesn't care if I pass out. He starts hammering into me with cruel strength, forcing me to take every inch of his big cock repeatedly, each stroke pushing me closer to the edge of ecstasy. The sound of the headboard slamming against the wall echoes in my ears, drowning out my strangled cries.

I can't fucking think. I can't even process the fact that we're playing with fire—that if anyone finds out he's ruining me like this, if anyone hears us, it's all over. It would destroy everything, end us both. But it seems like Rook is ready to risk it all for this moment. When I come again, my mind unravels, each wave of pleasure crashing through me like a violent storm.

And then, suddenly—the room is colder, his heat gone as he's ripped out of my pulsing pussy in the middle of our chaos. Before I can gather myself, I hear it—a loud crash. My eyes snap open, wide with panic.

The light flicks on, blinding, and my body moves instinctively, slamming my tied legs shut as I scramble to the side of the bed, pressing myself to the headboard. My heart races, but everything seems to move in slow motion as my gaze falls on him.

Rook. Standing there, his body coiled with tension, like a beast ready to pounce.

But it's not him who has my attention now. No, it's the man standing in front of him. My fucking dad. His chest rises and falls with each breath, fists clenched, wrath in his gaze. Tears sting my eyes, my heart hammering in my chest as I struggle against the Christmas lights, desperately trying to free my hands because I know—without a doubt—someone's going to die tonight.

CHAPTER FIVE

- PRESENT -

ROOK

After that night, everything fell apart. Ryker was involved, and I was told to leave Ebony behind—to "focus on other things and clear my head from my little sister," as he put it.

But not until I told her how I felt—how I really felt. And let's just say, that didn't go as planned. She made it very fucking clear she didn't feel the same, or at least, that's what she wanted me to believe.

And I did. So, I did what she asked.

I stayed the fuck away. I thought maybe, she'd miss me enough to reach out. A text, a call—something. But there was fuck all. Not a damn thing.

And with each silent day that passed, my frustration turned to hatred. Because I knew. I knew she wanted me just as much as I wanted her, but there was one massive difference—I was willing to burn the world down for her, and she wasn't.

Ebony is darkness wrapped in white silk. Perfect, polished, obedient on the outside to the man who pulls her strings, but beneath it all, there's a shadow inside her—a shadow that belongs only to me. It drives me insane how she lets him control her, how she always does as she's told, even when it breaks her inside.

Ryker gave me a choice that night: leave the city and disappear wherever the fuck he wanted or take a bullet between the eyes. I'm not scared of that motherfucker, or death for that matter, but when I spoke to Ebony and she gave me nothing to fight for, I knew it was time to go. I was too wrecked. I was spiraling out of control.

Now, I lead one of Ryker's new biker clubs just outside of the city. Drugs, alliances, weapons, murder—it's a regular thing. He turned me into a monster, the plague, twisted the knife until there was nothing left but violence. But I'll never fucking forget what he's done to me—to us. His time is coming, I have plans, and when it does, I'll burn everything he's built to the ground and laugh while doing it.

Ebony glances at me now and then with those pretty blue eyes. Alluring, always. Icier than Antarctica, yet hotter than the scorching boarders of hell. She knows I'm watching her, showing how I still want her and that I'm still sickly fucking obsessed with her. She knows me too well, the flame hasn't died, it's still there, burning bright and searing my dark soul.

We've got unfinished business. Unspoken words and before I leave here again, she's going to hear them. She's going to feel them. Fuck, I need her out of my system so fucking bad.

I lean over, dropping my cigarette in her champagne to annoy her and as it hisses, she gradually stands. She finally makes eye contact; a glare and I have to fight a grin. She drags her stare away from mine and passes me. My eyes follow her legs, gliding upward until they land on her round ass in that short dress. My jaw tightens, my teeth grinding as I think about eating that ass and pussy.

"Fuck," I hiss with anger, dropping my head as soon as she's out of sight, clearly going to use the restroom.

Don't do it, Rook. *Do not fucking do it.*

But I can't. I can't fucking stop myself; I'm weak for this little bitch. I sit back slightly, pulling my phone out. I swipe through it, finding my ringtones. As soon as I press play, the sound rings out and I stand. Then I pause it, pressing it to my ear. As I pretend to be on a call because I don't want us to be interrupted, I walk out, eyes briefly following me.

In the dimly lit corridor, I spot a single Christmas tree, decorated with warm lights, similar to the ones I used to tie her up with when I fucked her into oblivion. I lean against the wall next to it, taking in the different shaped ornaments until my eyes settle on one specific. It's black, shiny and drops down with a spiral design, almost like a unicorn horn. I raise an eyebrow until I hear the toilet flush from behind the door beside me and my attention sharpens.

As soon as the door unlocks and opens, I rest my head back. She passes me, her long hair swaying over her ass, but she doesn't get very far. I lunge forward, grabbing her wrist and whirl her around. My hand grabs her face swiftly, catching her off guard, my fingers digging into her jaw with a bruising force as I pin her against the wall.

Her breath hitches, shallow and uneven as Ouija, sleek and black as night, scales glinting like obsidian against the Christmas lights, coils herself around my tattooed wrist with a lazy elegance before slithering upward. She glides to the back of Ebony's neck, disappearing beneath her dark hair like a whispered threat.

Her body stiffens instantly, her fear lighting up those icy blue eyes, a spark I latch onto. I hold her gaze, watching as my small pet snake claims and violates her inch by inch, as if she belongs to us both.

"Stay very still, little sister," I murmur, the words dripping with control.

Ouija emerges again, winding down her chest toward the heavy curve of her cleavage, disappearing beneath her sparkly dress. Creeping beneath her big tit, I watch her curl herself around it, her movements are unhurried and agonizingly slow. Ebony holds her breath, and the silence of dread pulls my attention back to her wide eyes.

"Now," I say lowly, "lift that slutty dress and take off your panties."

Her eyes expand further, and she shakes her head slightly. "Are you fucking insane? Dad is right there. Are you trying to get us both killed?"

I lean closer, my breath brushing against her cheek. "Yeah, I fucking am," I mutter, my tone quiet but rich with danger. "Maybe I'm done hiding, Bunny. Maybe I don't give a fuck if we both burn for this. At least then, I'll have you. In life, in death—it doesn't fucking matter. Beyond these walls, beyond these chains, even in hell itself, you're mine."

Her eyes search mine as I draw back, the realization of my words settling between us. This isn't over, not even fucking close. "I'm not doing it, Rook. You need to—"

My fingers clench on her jaw, yanking her forward before slamming her head back against the wall with a sharp thud.

"Do it," I growl, my voice quiet but razor-sharp, my eyes blazing into hers.

"But Blaise—"

"Fuck. Blaise." The name rolls off my tongue like a death knell, dark and final, the possessiveness poisoning my veins. "You either do it, Eb, or I'll walk out there and tell Daddy I just fucked his daughter hard. Again. Get us both killed."

Her lips tremble, unshed tears glittering in her eyes, but I don't back off, keeping my mouth close to hers. She hesitates, then reaches down and lifts her tight dress over her hips. I tilt my chin upward in approval of her obedience. She hooks her thumbs beneath the strings and slides them down her thighs, never breaking eye contact.

The fabric hits her ankles, and my eyes flick to her lips—parted and glistening as she licks them. Leaning forward, I let my mouth brush hers, barely a kiss, just a spark to light the fire between us.

"Good girl," I bite out forcefully causing her body to jerk.

Ouija slithers higher, winding herself firmly around my wrist. When she settles where she belongs, my gaze drops to Ebony's panties—lacy and useless—bunched against her tall heels. A flicker of heat surges through my dick as I lower myself into a crouch, but her hand moves instinctively, tugging at her dress to cover herself.

I swat it away with a low growl, my warning clear, and her fingers curl into fists at her sides. My gaze roams over to her exposed perfect pussy, then I side-eye the living room door.

No movement.

I reach down, wrapping my hands around her ankles, lifting each one to peel the delicate lace free. For a second, she lets out a shallow breath, probably thinking that's all I wanted.

She's so fucking wrong.

The moment her panties are off, I'm on her. I dive in, my face buried between her thighs, my tongue plunging straight inside her cunt. Her sharp gasp slashes through the air as her hand flies to my hair, gripping tight. I don't stop. I glide upward, tasting every inch of her, parting her lips until I flick over her clit. Her legs buckle under my hold, and the instant her taste floods my mouth, I fucking lose it.

Fuck… My sisters pussy ain't supposed to be this damn good. This must be what pure sin tastes like.

I shoot to my feet, grabbing her face again, my lips hovering inches from hers as she pants in panic. Without a word, I shove her backward inside the bathroom. She stumbles as I release her, her heels clicking against the tile, and I reach for the tree without losing eye contact, yanking off that gleaming ornament without a second thought.

I follow her in, closing the door behind me and locking it with a final click.

"Rook—" she whispers harshly, her hands lifting in surrender. But I'm done playing these fucking games.

I stand there, breathing hard, my chest rising and falling, eyes wild as I lift a hand to my throat. Ouija slithers higher, coiling around me like she knows what's coming. As soon as she settles around my neck, I pounce.

I'm on her in a heartbeat, my hand wrapping around her throat, yanking her into me. Her gasp is muffled as I crash my lips against hers. My tongue forces its way past her lips and at first, she's stiff, her palms pressing weakly against my chest, but then she melts. Her resolve crumbles, and she kisses me back with just as much ferocity. Her hands tangle into the back of my hair, pulling me deeper into the blizzard of us.

I shift, dipping down and sliding my palms over the back of her thighs. With one swift motion, I hoist her effortlessly, her heels scraping my ass as she clings around me. The ornament dangles in my hand, its cold edge pressing into my palm as I drop her ass onto the sink.

My movements are hurried and rough as I yank the bust of her dress down, the fabric sliding away until her big tits bounce free. Breaking the kiss, I dip down without hesitation, wrapping my lips around her stiff nipple and suck hard. Her body jolts, a strangled gasp escaping her lips as I bite down just enough to make her squirm.

Shifting my hands behind her knees, I force her legs high and spread them wide. She leans back on one hand, leaving her completely open to me and my gaze drops to her pussy—bare, glistening, and fucking mine.

I lower myself with a growl, my tongue darting out and lashing at her with a cruel hunger. She lets out a sharp wheeze, her hand fisting in my hair as I devour her like a man possessed. My tongue moves furiously, gliding through her lips, flicking over her clit before plunging back inside her tight hole.

Her head falls back, her teeth sinking into her bottom lip as she struggles to hold back the moans threatening to spill free. But I don't stop. I won't stop, not until I've wrung every ounce of submission from her, her silent cries fueling the fire roaring between us.

As Ouija untangles from my throat, she slithers gracefully upward, coiling herself around Ebony's thigh. With my mouth still smothering her soaked pussy, my tongue and teeth working ruthlessly, I release her other leg. The thick, long and cold ornament is still clutched in my hand, its weight heavy with intent.

I quickly spit on the surface, before bringing it to her asshole. My lips seal over her clit, gnawing and sucking as I press the pointed tip against her. She glances down at me and my eyes flick upward to meet hers. Her brows are pinched in confusion, her mouth dropping open on a silent gasp.

The fight is brief as I twist the ornament, extending her inch by inch. Her body stiffens, her muscles taut beneath my grip. I push deeper, harder, watching as her expression morphs from shock to unrestrained pleasure.

Her head drops back again with a low, guttural growl. "Oh. My. Fuck," she hisses, her legs shuddering as strain coils through her body.

I don't go easy on her tight ring. I push the ornament into her, each thrust and rotation demanding her little hole to yield to the invasion. But as soon as her muscles give way and she's loose enough, I ram the entire thing inside her, over and over again wrecking her with a wicked force and pace, unable to stop myself. Her pink, stretched asshole swallows the black object repeatedly, gliding over its groves as if it belongs there, as if she was made the take the fucking thing.

My mouth never leaves her pussy. I devour her, my tongue flicking and exploring, drinking every drop of her arousal as it leaks. I nip at her swollen clit, suck it between my teeth, the taste of her sending me descending deeper into the abyss of her.

She starts hyperventilating, her big tits bouncing with each desperate, shuddering breath as the pleasure consumes her. I can feel it—feel the way her climax is building, the way her asshole sucks the object effortlessly inside her and my movements grow more violent, until she explodes. Her body jerks as she suppresses a scream, her pants broken as she fights for oxygen. Her pussy clenches, her asshole spasming in time, the aftermath rippling through her.

Even as she starts to tremble, I don't offer leniency. I push her further, fucking her ass harder until her legs shake and her body writhes, overwhelmed by the punishing overstimulation.

I give her one final lick, gathering her sweet come on my tongue, cherishing her taste before ripping the ornament out of her ruined asshole with a final, harsh yank.

As more come leaks from her pussyhole, dribbling onto the tiled floor, I rise between her quivering legs, my eyes trail up her beautiful body. She's a masterpiece of mess—head flung back, tits heaving, eyes still closed as she struggles to come back down to earth.

I raise an expressionless eyebrow, but satisfaction curls in my chest, even as the ache in my cock and balls becomes almost unbearable. As I stare at her, I place a firm hand on her hip and Ouija coils herself snugly around my arm again, a silent witness to the destruction I've left in my wake. My free hand tangles in the back of Ebony's hair, gripping a handful and her dazed eyes finally flutter open.

I lower my mouth to hers, our lips touching as I whisper, "I'll see you real soon, my bunny."

Her eyes scan mine, still glazed with the impact of what I just did to her, but she doesn't say a word and her silence says enough. I press a soft, lingering kiss to her plump lips before stepping back, my fingers releasing her hair. But as soon as I place my hand on the door handle, a knock hits the wood.

"Ebony are you okay in there?" my mom's voice calls from the other side of the door.

I roll my eyes, my teeth biting in annoyance, while Ebony bolts into action. She jumps off the sink in a panic, her movements frantic as she scrambles to pull herself together.

"I'm okay, Cind!" she shouts, her voice high-pitched as she yanks her dress down, smoothing the fabric with her hands.

Her wide eyes flick to mine, then, with a hasty breath, she blurts out, "I don't suppose you have any pads here?"

I smirk slightly, enjoying every second of her discomfort and glance at the door again.

"I might. Let me check!"

I hear the sharp click of my mom's heels retreating, fading into the distance, and I turn to face Eb. She's standing in front of the mirror now, her eyes cold and distant as she smooths down her clothes, restoring herself to the image of what she believes is perfection. But there's nothing perfect in the air between us.

I move behind her, my presence a reminder of how filthy with sin she really is. I'm an unremovable stain. Always will be.

"You were so much more flawless when you were a mess for me," I murmur, grazing against the shell of her ear. "You come like a demon but taste like an angel, little sister."

She rolls her eyes, the only defense left in her, before shaking her head and turning to meet my gaze.

"This has to stop. We both know it," she whispers, a thread of hesitation in her voice, but I know her too well.

"You weren't saying that a fucking second ago," I counter, "when I had my tongue buried inside your cunt, while I wrecked your ass with a Christmas tree ornament."

Her eyes widen, her cheeks burning red, but I close the space between us in a single stride until my lips glide over hers as she tips her head back, my breath hot.

"You can pretend all you want, act like a prim, proper princess for everyone else, Eb. But for me? I know you. The real you. The dirty you. You'll always be that little slut—greedy, desperate, wanting nothing more than to be filled by your big brother's cock."

Her breath catches in her throat, her eyes showing she's caught somewhere between defiance and something darker, something she can't deny.

"You'll never fucking escape this. You'll never escape me. And this Christmas? You'll see exactly how far I'll go…" My teeth sink together, the words biting from my mouth, "To. Destroy. You."

She breathes heavily, her eyes scanning mine before slanting them and I continue.

"Let's see how you like to be used," I exhale, and her brows pinch slightly.

"Used?" she repeats, her whisper sharp but wavering. "You fucked me once… When is it ever enough for you, Rook? You got what you wanted. You can't just walk back into my life and demand—"

"Did I?" I cut her off, lifting a brow. "If I remember correctly, I broke you in. I gave you more orgasms than you could count in mere minutes. But did I *claim* you? No. I never got to fill you with my fucking cum." My voice dips, turning cruel. "I was dragged out of your tight pussy before I could even take what was mine."

Her throat bobs as she swallows hard, her expression hardening. "And whose fault was that?" she bites back, her eyes warning me. "You told me to be quiet, and I did, despite the pain. I stayed silent until you couldn't help yourself—until you fucked me so violently, I thought you were giving me organ damage."

The memory slams into me like a wrecking ball, vivid, scorching, every sinful detail replaying in my head like a sensual masterpiece. I can't hold back the growl rumbling from my chest, my dick tingling with that same overwhelming sensation when I think about it. The best night of my life, and it was taken away too soon.

"That was nothing," I snarl, a wicked grin tugging at my lips, my voice thick with malice. "Nothing compared to what I want to do to you now." I lean closer and her body stiffens. "I'm not the boy I was back then. I'm a man now. You thought I was rough then? I'm now a man with a seriously fucked-up imagination. And judging by the way you just handled that Christmas horn thing—oh, little sister, you're not the sweet, innocent girl I once knew either. You're a fucking anal slut."

Her eyes flash with disobedience, her chin lifting in a desperate show of control as she crosses her arms tightly over her chest, so I press closer to deliver the final blow.

"Daddy will never know his perfect daughter likes to screw her ass with a big, pink dildo and has learned how to squirt when she climax's." My whisper is lethal, a dark secret drawn into the light.

Her defiance shatters in an instant. Her face falls, her blue eyes widening in disbelief as realization sinks in—I've been fucking watching. I've been stalking her, scrutinizing her every dirty secret, peeling back the faultless mask she hides behind.

"You always get your laptop so wet, Eb. Sometimes I wonder how the fuck it survives with all that come you spray over it."

She blinks at me, blankly, like her mind is struggling to process my sickening words, then, with sneer, I murmur, "What's that Christmas song? You know the one…" I pause before my voice drops as I sing darkly, "*I watch you when you're sleeping. I know when you're awake. I know if you've been bad or good… so be good, for goodness' sake.*"

"You sick fuck," she seethes, and her fury is intoxicating, but the way her voice trembles with shame and humiliation is even better. This is us, who we used to be, and I relish the back-and-forth bullshit.

I grin, biting my pierced bottom lip as my eyes move down her body, a sweep that leaves no part of her untouched by my hungry gaze. When I look at her again, I see it—fright, anger, arousal—a cocktail of emotions she can't hold.

"Only for you, sis," I murmur as I throw in a wink. "But please don't ever be a fucking good for me. I like it when you're a bad girl. My naughty list… Fuck, it's only growing longer for you, bunny. Your name is printed all over it. Tell me." I add, my voice a seductive, dark whisper edged with menace. "When are you're going to sit on my knee… I mean, cock."

Her eyes squint, her jaw tightening, and for a second, I see the spark of the girl I used to know—my sister—who would never back down from a challenge when we were alone, who always rose to my annoying taunts like they were a goad she couldn't refuse.

She looks like she's gonna fucking fight me, like she's itching to go at it the way we did when we were younger. Back then, it was all harmless—just me provoking her until she snapped, and then she'd throw herself at me with an anger that could make anyone believe she stood a chance. But she never won. Not once. I'd always pin her down, holding her squirming body until she gave up or screamed in frustration.

But now? Now it's different. She knows better than to attack me, knows exactly what would happen if she did. Because if I pinned her down now, it wouldn't stop there. No, she'd be pinned down and fucked. Hard. Only screaming for more.

Suddenly, there's a sharp knock at the door, and my mom's voice seeps through the wood.

"Got some!"

Ebony pushes against my chest, forcing me back. I move sluggishly, my body reluctant, until I'm hidden behind the door. She side-eyes me, then takes a deep, steadying breath before reaching for the handle. Her face transforms instantly, that fake smile slipping into place as she opens it.

"Oh, thank you!" she chirps, her voice laced with forced sweetness, taking the pads from my mom's outstretched hand.

She moves to close the door, but my mom stops her with a hand pressed firmly against it and Ebony freezes, her posture rigid.

"Have you seen Rook?"

Ebony shakes her head slightly and lifts her chin. "No," she replies smoothly. "I've been in here."

My mom hesitates, the silence between uncomfortable. "Oh," she says finally. "He must still be on the phone."

There's a beat of tension before she speaks again, "wait, is that one of the Christmas tree ornaments?"

My eyes flick to it lying on the floor and the temptation to smirk claws at me, but I stop myself. I watch as Ebony glances back at it, her movements stiff. "Hm," she says, her voice light but strained. "It must be. I'll bring it out in a second."

The silence that follows is stifling, heavy with suspicion. I can almost hear my mom questioning everything, the gears in her head turning, but finally, she leaves. As the door closes, Ebony's shoulders drop, her body slackening with relief.

Without hesitation, she bends down, snatching up the ornament. Straightening, she moves to the sink, her steps rushed, her expression tight with irritation. She scrubs it under the tap, her head shaking with frustration. She doesn't even look at me. It's like I'm not even here anymore, like I don't fucking exist.

When she's finished, she dries it, then without a word, without even glancing my way, she unlocks the door and walks out, her anger clear in the air she leaves behind.

I stay still for a moment, the sound of the closing door echoing in the silence. Slowly, I let my head fall back against the wall, my eyes slipping shut as my hand drags over the stubble on my jaw. I exhale heavily, her cold persona settling in my gut. My hand falls limply to my side, my head dipping forward as defeat starts to hit me all over again.

CHAPTER SIX

Sitting on the couch with Cindy, I pull my dark hair forward, letting it cascade over my shoulder as she fastens the necklace she bought me.

Her fingers work delicately, the clasp clicking into place. When she's done, I glance down at it—a small token of kindness in the madness—and then swivel to face her, giving a soft, grateful smile.

"Thank you," I say, my voice quiet, but genuine.

Before she can respond, the air changes. Rook strides into the room, his vibe demanding attention as always. He doesn't spare me a look as he moves toward the kitchen, but my eyes follow him instinctively, drawn like a moth to a flame I should know better than to touch.

And then I feel it—a piercing gaze. My stomach constricts, panic winding inside me as I realize my dad is watching me. His stare is heavy, probing, challenging, a clear warning until finally, he looks away.

My focus snaps back to Rook as he downs a glass of whiskey in one smooth motion, the tension in his posture showing he's agitated. I watch him grab his helmet off the counter, preparing to leave already and my heart rate spikes. Cindy notices right away and she's on her feet in seconds, hurrying toward him. I stay where I am, rooted to the couch, unsure whether to say goodbye or let him go without a word.

This is what we've become. Awkward. Fractured. Our once-normal—well, normal-ish—family life now a tangled mess of avoiding each other or forbidden lust. We're like a spreading blemish, dark and poisonous, infecting everything around us. And no matter how much time or distance keeps us apart; the rot doesn't fade. It just lingers. It festers into something so much fucking worse.

My eyes fix on him, the vivid flashbacks in my mind. The way he just manhandled me in that bathroom, lifting and dropping me down with a grip that stole my breath, taking exactly what he wants. The way he fucked my ass with that ornament, his tongue annihilating me at the same time, pulling muffled sounds from me that didn't belong in this world.

It's clear as day. Rook still has me, body and soul, wrapped around his little finger. And no matter how far he walks away, how many years he leaves, no matter how much I want to avoid us, I'll never be free. And I know that now more than ever since he's clearly been hacking my shit and watching me. *Psycho.*

I've thought about it for years, wondering if fate would've been kinder, if life had played out differently. If he hadn't been my brother, would our souls have still found their way to one another? Could we have had the freedom to love without the judgment crushing us? Without the watching eyes, the whispers, the smothering control?

People don't understand the agony of it—loving someone so deeply and knowing they're right there in front of you, so close you can feel them, but being stopped from reaching for them.

Cindy leans in, pressing a kiss to his cheek, her voice soft, her smile beaming. He then walks toward the door without stopping, without looking at me. Just like that, he's gone, leaving me wondering when I'll see him again and it feels like the air's been sucked out of the room.

I lower my head, closing my eyes as the ache in my chest spreads. It's the same old feeling, familiar in the worst way. My hands tremble on my thighs, and I press them into fists to make it stop. The sting behind my eyes grows sharper, hotter. Feeling like I've lost him all over again. Lost the other part of me.

I need to get the fuck out of here.

I tug on my jacket as I stand, then sling my bag over my shoulder and make my way toward the kitchen. My dad's eyes are waiting for me as I step inside, suspicious and calculating. His gaze rakes over me like he's looking for flaws, anything out of place.

"I'm going to see Blaise," I say, forcing the words out calmly.

I see the flicker of pride in his expression when I say his name, like it's a currency he's fucking collecting. But his pride is worth nothing to me anymore. Not like it used to be. It's just another leash, another way to wrap me up in the life I'm slowly suffocating in.

"Merry Christmas, Ebony," he says, stepping forward to press a kiss to my forehead.

"Merry Christmas, Dad," I answer, my voice barely above a whisper. But as I turn to leave, he suddenly snatches my upper arm and yanks me into him.

"Stay the fuck away from him," he warns with a growl in my ear.

He hovers for a beat, and I stare ahead, blank, my heart pounding. When he lets me go, I stay in the same spot a second longer, my jaw tight until I walk away, making my way to my car outside.

Noel of Sin

The cold hits me as soon as I step outside, snow drifting around me like fragile whispers in the dark. I pull my arm tighter across my chest with a frustrated growl, digging through my bag for my keys and each quick step feels like a reminder of what Rook did to me in that damn bathroom.

As soon as I climb inside, I turn the heater on full blast and pull the seatbelt over me before driving away. I head toward Blaise's apartment, but my mind is a mess. I don't plan to stay, I never do. Just dinner like promised, then leave to be on my own this Christmas. But I can't get Rook out my head. He's somewhere in the same city as me and it feels like I can sense him in the air. Like a shadow following me.

I turn the music on, trying to clear my thoughts, my fingers tapping on the steering wheel mindlessly but it's all a blur. Every moment is filled with his face, his perfect body flashing through my mind. How he feels between my legs. The heaviness of his big cock inside me. Then I start thinking about how I've never given him head before and I'd like too.

"Fuck. Stop." I mutter to myself, adjusting in my seat, feeling my thighs are sticky, my pussy still bare.

Next thing I know, I'm outside Blaise's block and I park up. As I cut the engine, I take a deep breath, steadying myself before finally getting out of the car.

Noel of Sin

I step off the elevator on the top floor and make my way down the long hallway, fingers running through my hair. When I reach the door at the end, I hesitate for a moment, my hand hovering before finally knocking my knuckles against the black wood.

"It's open!" Blaise's deep voice echoes from inside.

I turn the handle and step in, immediately taking in the massive space. Blaise might run the Shadow Serpents MC here in Boston, but "small time" is what people say. Looking around at the sleek black walls, the towering ceilings, and the high-end furnishings, it's clear he's anything but. The apartment screams modern wealth—sharp, dark, and elegant, with touches of Christmas decorating every corner. A massive 10-foot black tree dominates the center of the living room, standing tall in front of the huge floor-to-ceiling windows that overlook the city's twinkling skyline.

I move deeper into the apartment, hearing him in the kitchen, off to the right. My steps feel heavy as I make my way toward him, the usual reluctance sinking into my stomach.

When I round the corner, I catch sight of him setting down plates on the kitchen island, steam rising from a pan on the stove and I stop, observing him carefully. Blaise is tall and built—muscular, tatted up, wearing a tight black shirt and pants that show off his frame.

His long black hair is tied back in a messy manbun, and the stubble along his jaw sharpens the edges of his face. He's older than me—closer to the age where men think about settling down, I guess. My dad swears Blaise has his life together. Says he'll look after me. But to be honest, I always find myself comparing every guy I date to my brother. It's a fucked-up compulsion I can't shake.

His piercing blue eyes suddenly meet mine as he leans over the island and a small smirk tugs at his lips. He walks toward me and when he is close enough, he leans down, pressing a kiss to my cold cheek. My jaw tenses instinctively, but when he withdraws, I give a small smile.

"Looking beautiful as always." He says, a brow raised.

I would probably be flattered if this wasn't a forced arrangement, although I don't know it is on his behalf, maybe it's just business, but it's certainly not genuine either way. Blaise is a hot guy, he's clearly loaded, he's mature, but he just doesn't give that spark. He can't erase the deeply rooted feelings I have for Rook. I don't think anyone can.

He moves around me, slipping off my jacket before placing his hand low on my back, guiding me to the island where the food is. I take a seat, slipping onto the barstool, my eyes fixed on the plate in front of me.

As he sits beside me, where he can see me, I feel his greedy eyes sweeping over me, but I don't lift mine. I know what he wants. It's what they always want. And every time I come here; I feel it more intensely. He wants to fuck me, but I won't let him. I'm not prepared to jump in bed with a guy I barely know. Like it's going to magically appear a fucking connection that's just not there.

I told myself, if he keeps at it, if he somehow wins me over, then maybe I'll give him what he wants. But if not, I'll ask my dad to move on to the next. I'll buy as much time as I can before I'm cornered with what's coming. Marriage. Kids. Tying families together. Building bridges.

But not for me. Not for my sake. Because that's all I am, right? Just a pawn in everyone else's game, moving toward whatever will give them more power. My happiness means fuck all.

I lift my fork and dig in, feeling his need wrapping around me, much more tightly tonight than I have ever felt when I've come here. Blaise is waiting—expectant, like tonight's the night I'm just going to hand my pussy over to him like some pretty fucking gift because it's Christmas.

At least when I gave myself to Rook, it wasn't like this. I knew him. All of him. I watched that boy grow into a man. I saw the flaws, the darkness, the light. The tears. The pain. The joy. I witnessed it all. I knew him inside out, just as he knew me. I trusted him with my life, and that's why I gave him everything. My innocence, my body, my heart.

No one else was ever going to compare to that connection. Brother or not, I didn't fucking care anymore. I loved him too much to let anyone taint that night. Yeah, it caused an uproar, but it's ours. No one can take it away from us. It's solidified in stone and engraved in our souls.

It's just… Complicated.

As I take a bite of food, chewing slowly, I start thinking about the first time he ever ramped up the tension between us and the first time I caved. It was the year before we fucked in that cabin, when he took my virginity. It was Christmas eve, and I had been ice-skating on the lake near our home...

CHAPTER SEVEN

- FLASHBACK -

ROOK

It's Christmas Eve, and I'm standing outside Ebony's bedroom door. I'd just returned from spending the evening with the girl I'm dating and her family—a pointless, suffocating situation I found myself in. Forced small talk, fakeness. I barely even remember their fucking faces because they don't mean anything.

The second I walked through the front door; my mom dropped the bombshell. Bunny had an accident. She fell through the ice on the lake while skating. The lake we've been around our whole lives. My heart stopped for a second when she said it, my mind spinning with images of her beneath the ice, cold and struggling. They said she's fine. *Fine*. But I know Bunny better than anyone in this damn house or world and she's never fine if something like that happens.

And no one fucking called me. That's what burns because no motherfuck in our lives understands what she means to me, even if I know they shouldn't anyway. That's the fucked-up truth.

I stand there, staring at the door, my hand on the cold handle. I shouldn't go in. I know I shouldn't, but I can't stop. I never can when it comes to her. If I had my way, I would be around her all day, every day, but it's becoming harder lately, my will breaking.

I gently press the handle down, and the door creaks open just enough for me to slip inside. It's dark, the only light coming from the heavy snowfall outside, casting a pale, ghostly glow through her window. The room is quiet, except for the faint sound of her shaky breathing.

There she is. Ebony, curled beneath the floral duvet, her back to me. She's shivering, trembling so hard I can see it from across the room. I close the door softly, feeling my pulse in my ears, thudding harder as I step closer to her.

I shrug off my leather jacket, tossing it over the chair, then stride around the bed, stopping to stare down at her. She's tucked the duvet tightly under her chin, as if she's trying to shield herself from the cold.

I crouch, and she suddenly stops breathing all together, as if she knows it's me. I reach out, gently moving a lock of her shiny black hair away that clings to her thick lashes, her soft skin cold and pale.

"You good?" I whisper as I always do when it's us alone, like we're a fucking secret that no one can know about.

Her eyes gently open until her piercing blue orbs are on mine. She scans over my features before closing them again, pulling the duvet further around her.

"I'm so cold, Rook. It's rattling my bones," she murmurs through chattering teeth. "Nothing I do will warm me up."

I sigh before standing and then hop onto the bed behind her. I slip under the duvet, and she turns her head, warily.

"What are you doing? You can't..."

"Take your clothes off Bunny." I order in hushed tones.

She freezes completely. "What?" She breathes.

"You heard. Take your fucking clothes off." I repeat.

"But…"

"Eb, I've seen you in your underwear and swimwear, stop it. I'm your brother."

I know why she's hesitating, and I know I'm stupid for putting both of us in such a scenario, this warped fucking scenario that's going to test the life out of me but right now, it's purely to warm her the fuck up, nothing else. I tell myself.

I watch carefully as she slips out of her Christmas pajamas beneath the duvet. As soon as she's in just her bra and panties, she glances over at me and I reach over, wrapping my arm around her back and yank her closer me. She's stiff under my touch as her front presses against mine.

I reach down, lifting my shirt and give a head gesture, "Get under."

She pauses for a second, thinking carefully until finally, she slips her head under, the reluctant clear in her movements and I pull it down her back. Holding her close to me, her almost naked body on mine sends me into a frenzy. My warmth seeps into her, her shivering starting to ease as she just breathes.

"How was your night with Jessica," she asks in a whisper, her words muffled but not enough for me not to hear her.

I don't answer. I know it gets under her skin when I date girls just to fuck her out of my system. Although, it doesn't seem to work. It's gotten even harder now she's getting older. She's beautiful and attracting attention from guys. Even my friends. The number of guys I've had to beat the fuck up or almost kill is stupid, and she might think it's just natural brotherly instincts, but it's not.

It's far beyond that. It's fucking possessiveness and jealousy like nothing I have ever felt before. Something dangerous. I'd murder a motherfucker for my sister, but not in the way you're supposed to, in a way because she's fucking mine. *Only mine.*

I lift my collar and slip my head beneath my shirt, instantly feeling the warmth of her face and breath mingling with mine. She ceases inhaling all together from the close proximity. Although we've never said it to one another, I know she feels the same way. She brushes it off, but she knows.

As her plump lips lightly touch mine, I slip my hand beneath my shirt and slide it over her bare hip, then the curve of her ass, torturing myself.

"I'd rather be here," I whisper. "With you."

"Rook…" she says, warning me, but I can't stop.

I was stupid enough to come in here and now her body is so soft, so perfect against mine, it's making me rock solid already. I can't think straight. My sanity is crumbling. When I reach the back of her thigh, I lift it, wrapping it around my waist and she exhales a shaky breath.

"I'm just trying to warm you up." I fucking lie.

My palm slides up the back of her thigh again until my fingers are slipping beneath her panties, landing on her ass and I give it a tight squeeze causing her to hiss, her body bucking against me.

My hand moves up her back causing a shiver to run through her, until it's under her hair and on the nape of her neck. She reluctantly moves too, her fingers skim over my abs, and I can feel our sense of control slipping quickly.

"I've never…"

"I know, Eb, I know." I cut her off, knowing she's never touched a guy let alone kissed them, I've made sure of it, yet here we are, shattering everything about our sibling relationship. But I've wanted nothing more than this. Than her.

One of her hands glides up my pec until it's wrapped around the back of my neck, drawing me even closer to her mouth.

"Will you teach me how to kiss?" she murmurs, her breath warm and soft against my lips, the words a whisper that threads through the air between us, making my pulse quicken.

For a moment, I freeze, wondering if I heard her right.

"No," her voice trembles, trying to retreat, "Maybe…" she whispers, but I won't let her slip away now.

Without hesitation, I close the distance, slamming my lips against hers, taking the moment—taking her. She goes still, caught off guard, and then, she begins to kiss me back, that first tentative touch sparking something inside me. A fire. A fucking hunger. I press firmer and her tense body against mine, somehow starts to... surrender.

My hand moves up, settling around her throat, the grip gentle but possessive. I break the kiss, just enough to murmur, "Open your mouth. Move your tongue and lips with mine. Let me show you what this really fucking means."

I don't wait for an answer, I'm on her again, but this time, my tongue slips past her lips. Hers meets mine, hesitant at first, but then she responds, matching my urgency as if we've been here before. Our mouths move in perfect sync, her body giving way to mine, yielding to the dark pull between us. I can feel her—feel every breath, every tremor—as I dominate her lips, coaxing her to follow.

Her hand rakes through back of my hair, pulling me closer, deeper. I lean over her, forcing her back against the pillow, and my thigh presses against her warm pussy, grinding with just enough pressure to make her gasp. She bucks against it, desperate, hungry and I feel like I'm losing my fucking mind.

I take her hand, guiding it downward, slipping it beneath the edge of her panties. My voice is low, rough, like a warning, "Touch your pussy for me, little sister. Show me how you get off when no one is watching, then kiss me like it's my hand pleasuring you."

She hesitates, breath catching, but I slip my hand inside too, placing my hand over hers, forcing her fingers to move, to rub and explore her pussy. The heat of her hand under mine is almost too much, and when she moans, I feel the tension coil tighter between us. Her fingers find the rhythm, moving with growing urgency, and I can't look away, can't stop watching as she gives herself over to it, to me.

"Fuck, you're so lucky you're my sister or I'd be pounding my cock inside this little cunt right now," I growl lowly.

CHAPTER EIGHT

- PRESENT -

Ebony

Yeah, I came. He didn't know then, but it was the first time I ever came. Then he cuddled me until I fell asleep before sneaking back to his room. After that sinful night between us, everything spiraled. He started to lose his damn mind.

While my dad was in his club, taking care of business, Rook laid me on the back seat of my dad's car, lifted my skirt and ate my pussy out. There were a few odd occasions where we kissed again, but I started pulling away, it was becoming riskier and I knew he could never be mine, no matter how much I wanted him.

It had been around five months, and I thought we was getting past things, even if our relationship was straining and becoming difficult, we hadn't touched or kissed, until of course, that

Christmas in the cabin when everything came crashing down and we both cracked.

Suddenly, Blaise places a black box down beside me, and my heart skips a beat—not from excitement, but from a dread that pulls me out of my forbidden thoughts. I lift my eyes to his, keeping my expression neutral, and he responds with a slight, smug smirk.

Please don't be an engagement ring. For fuck's sake.

I let my fork clatter to the plate and reach for the box. My fingers tug at the silky black bow, letting it unravel and fall limply onto the counter. As I lift the lid, my eyes immediately fall on the object inside.

"I had it made in China for you," Blaise says, his tone almost eager, the opposite to the usual detached authority he carries.

My brows knit together as I take in the black-and-gold design, the Chinese markings unfamiliar. "Is it for hair?" I ask, the confusion clear in my voice.

He snickers softly, standing from the stool with an unsettling ease. Without answering, he plucks the object from the box and moves behind me. My hands drop to my lap as I stare ahead, while he gathers the top half of my black hair.

"I always wonder what your face looks like when your hair isn't always falling messily over it," he mutters. "Your eyes are far too pretty to keep hidden."

The clip snaps into place with a metallic click, and he steps back around, returning to his seat. This time, though, he angles his body toward me, the stool creaking softly under his weight as he leans in closer—too close.

I avoid his gaze, focusing intently on the fork I'd put down, but then his hand finds my chin. His fingers are firm as they guide my face upward, forcing me to look at him.

"What do you say?" he asks, his tone dripping with arrogance, as if he's speaking to a fucking child who needs a lesson in manners.

I swallow the irritation rising in my throat, shoving it down where it can't betray me and my voice is flat, cold, just the way he deserves.

"Thank you, Blaise."

For a moment, he observes me, his eyes lingering on mine as if searching for a lie. Then, he guides me to his lips and when they touch, his kiss is forceful, but I barely respond. The lack of reciprocation doesn't go unnoticed, and I see it in his eyes—a flicker of frustration in his expression, his jaw tightens. He drops his hand, but his face remains close, and his gaze roams down my body, lingering on my tits like he's not going to take no for an answer.

"I want to see you wearing nothing but that hairpiece for me tonight, Ebony," he says, his tone brooking no argument. "It's going to glitter so prettily as I take your pussy from behind."

My eyes flutter closed, and I feel my heart hammering against my ribs until I feel his warm, large hand wrap around my bare inner thigh. My eyes snap open, my body stiffening and when his palm moves upward, pushing under my dress, I act quickly, grabbing his wrist.

But Blaise is strong—too strong. His fingers graze my bare pussy, sending a jolt of anger and disgust through my veins before I manage to shove him away. The rejection lands like a physical blow, and I see it beyond his usual calm façade. His eyes blaze, the intensity of a storm swirling in the space between us.

"You know I own you, right?" he breathes, his voice low and malicious, a warning lacing each syllable.

I arch a brow, refusing to back down. "Oh yeah? And who made you believe that? Because it sure as hell wasn't me."

His lips curl slightly, mockingly and the smirk alone feels like a rope tightening around my neck.

"Do you really think you have a choice? Three months, Ebony. You keep coming here. You keep meeting me. You keep giving me your time, pretending to play coy. You're not just mine—you're fucking trapped."

The words strike me, stealing the air from my lungs. I feel the sting of tears burning at the corners of my eyes, but I fight them, trying not to break. His hand tightens on my thigh, the pressure bordering on painful, as his other hand tangles in the back of my hair, pulling tight, forcing my gaze to meet his.

"And what's mine does as they're fucking told," he says, his tone terrifyingly relaxed as his eyes scan mine. "I've given you more than enough time to grow the fuck up."

A single tear slips free, hot and unwelcome as it traces a path down my cheek. It's not fear—no. I don't fear Blaise or any other man. Only my father has ever earned that power over me. But the truth in his words is like salt being poured into an open wound. Another man here to control me. To use me. And once again, I'm left with no escape, no choice.

I compose myself, swallowing the bitter taste of my vulnerability, and force my voice into a shaky whisper.

"You'd better be careful who you're speaking to like that, motherfucker. Get your stubby ass fingers off me."

His grin returns and he leans in, his breath warm against my skin, his words quiet and deadly. "We're going to get married, Ebony. And you're going to give me sons—one after the fucking other—until your pussy gives out. That's the only reason I want you," he pauses, letting the insult settle in before continuing. "Beyond your looks and that gift between your legs? You're nothing. A weak, mind-numbing runt."

Rage floods my veins so quickly I barely register the red haze that clouds my vision. Before I can think, I gather spit in my mouth and release it sharply straight into his eye.

"Fuck!" Blaise recoils, letting me go instantly to wipe it away, and I don't waste a second. I leap off the stool, fueled by adrenaline, and dart toward the counter where my coat is.

But he's quick—too quick. His hand clamps around my arm with bruising force, his fingers digging into my skin.

"Not so fast," he growls.

I don't hesitate. My hand flies out, finding the nearest weapon—the hot frying pan still on the stove. Without warning, I spin and swing it with every ounce of strength I have. The impact is sickening, a metallic crack against the side of his head. Blaise collapses instantly, a grunt of pain escaping him as he hits to the floor, holding his face.

I stand over him, my breath heaving, tears streaming down my cheeks. My hands tremble, but beneath the anger and hurt, there's something else—a flicker of control, rare and unfamiliar, surging through me. Expressionless, I toss the frying pan carelessly, aiming for his nuts. It lands with a satisfying thunk between his legs, and he howls in fresh agony, curling into himself like a wounded animal.

"Merry fucking Christmas, pig," I say, my tone cold, detached, and turn on my heel. I grab my coat and bag, ignoring his groans behind me, and stride out of the apartment.

Noel of Sin

The chill of the night, snowy air hits my face as I step onto the street, but I barely feel it. I'm too busy wiping the tears from my cheeks, my chest constricting with uneven breaths. For the first time in what feels like forever, I don't feel like a damn puppet—I feel alive.

I slide into the car, slamming the door behind me, my breath fogging the icy interior. The key turns in the ignition with a metallic growl, the engine sputtering to life. From the corner of my eye, I catch a glimpse of Blaise exiting the building, his figure stark against the snow swirling in the air. I don't even glance in his direction. Instead, I grip the wheel tightly and pull away, the tires spinning briefly on the slippery ground before catching.

The snow falls heavier by the second, thickening the air and muffling the world around me. My headlights carve narrow tunnels through the storm, but the roads ahead are a ghostly blur, empty and unfamiliar. I have no destination, no plan, just the instinct to get the fuck away from here.

I can't go back to my place—not yet. My dad will find out, and his reaction could go one of two ways: lose his mind at me or kill Blaise. Either scenario feels equally exhausting, and on

Christmas Eve, I can't be bothered with either. So, I just drive, aimlessly, letting the road unfold in front of me.

Before long, the Christmassy city fades into the rearview mirror, replaced by winding, white-draped backroads leading into the woods. The trees press in on either side, their dark forms blurred by the relentless snowfall. The farther I go, the more I feel the pull of isolation, the hum of the tires blending with the sound of my ragged breaths.

Then it happens—a flicker on the dash, a red light blinking urgently. *Low gas.*

I frown, my brows knitting in confusion. How the hell is that possible? I thought I had almost a full tank when I left Blaise's apartment.

Shifting in my seat, I glance at the gauge, my heartbeat quickening as the needle sinks lower with each mile. It doesn't make sense, but there's no time to question it. My focus sharpens to now finding a gas station, but the snowy backroads extend endlessly, winding further into the unknown.

The unavoidable happens far too soon. The engine stammers, a jarring cough, and then silence. The car glides forward sluggishly before I steer it to the side of the road. My hands slam against the wheel, a growl of frustration ripping from my throat.

The road is deserted, the world silent and still. I glance around, the eerie glow of a single streetlight illuminating the otherwise pitch-black area. The snow glistens beneath it, falling in hypnotic swirls, blanketing the road. I grip the wheel, my chest tightening. Alone, in the middle of nowhere, on Christmas Eve.

Great. Just fucking great.

I reach for my bag on the passenger seat, fingers fumbling for my phone. My thumb hovers over my dad's number, instinct kicking in. He's who I'd normally call in an emergency. But tonight, I hesitate.

Instead, I swipe to another name—Rook. My breath stops as I stare at it, his name glowing against the dim light of the screen. The rational part of me knows better, but desperation wins out and with a shaky exhale, I press call.

The phone goes to my ear, the cold surface chilling my skin, but all I hear is an empty beep before the line cuts out.

Fuck.

I lower the phone, frustration bubbling, only to notice the signal bar glaring back at me—empty. My jaw clenches as I toss the phone onto the seat, then lean back for my boots on the floor behind me. Pulling them free, I kick off my heels, their delicate straps useless for the icy road. Slowly, I lace up the boots around my legs and once I'm ready, I grab my phone and push open the door. The night greets me with a freezing bite, the snow falling in thick, heavy flakes. It clings to my hair, my fur jacket, but I ignore it, keeping my head down.

The stillness presses against me as I circle to the front of the car, my eyes glued to the signal bar, waving the phone uselessly in the air. Nothing. No bars, no movement.

I glance up, scanning the deserted road. No headlights, no distant hum of an engine. No one.

Then, I feel something uneasy creep up my spine suddenly, and I look the other way.

Beneath the streetlight, a tall, shadowy figure stands still, bold against the falling snow. My breath holds as my eyes fix on them.

They don't move, don't acknowledge me, just stand there, letting the snow pile on their broad frame.

My brows knit, confusion warring with anxiety. Who the hell would be out here this late, on Christmas Eve, in the middle of nowhere? A thought flickers through my mind—maybe they can help. Maybe they have a phone with signal.

"Hey!" I call out, my voice cutting through the muffled quiet of the snow.

The figure doesn't move as my boots crunching in place before I start trudging toward him, each step sinking deeper into the white blanket beneath me. The air grows colder, and heavier, the world narrowing to just the two of us. As I close the distance, the snowfall thins, and I can see him more clearly.

And then I freeze a few feet away.

He stands with his back to me, his posture unnervingly still, as if my presence barely registers. My gaze travels up his form—a pair of black, laced boots planted firmly in the snow, tight black jeans tucked into them, and a black leather jacket with a hood pulled over his head. Silver cursive embroidery gleams across his back, catching the faint light: *The Plague.*

A ripple of anxiety coils in my stomach.

"Could you help me, sir?" I try again, my voice wobbling despite my attempt to sound calm. "I need a phone. I can't get signal here…"

For a moment, there's nothing but silence. Then his gloved hands drop to his sides. One of them holds a long black cane, the shaft wrapped in white, flashing Christmas lights spiraling upward in a twisted mockery of holiday cheer.

Before I can process the bizarre detail, he moves. His head jerks sharply to the side, and I catch my first glimpse of his face—or what's covering it.

A black matte mask, its surface smooth and shining, with a long, curved beak protruding outward and hollow eye sockets.

The plague doctor mask.

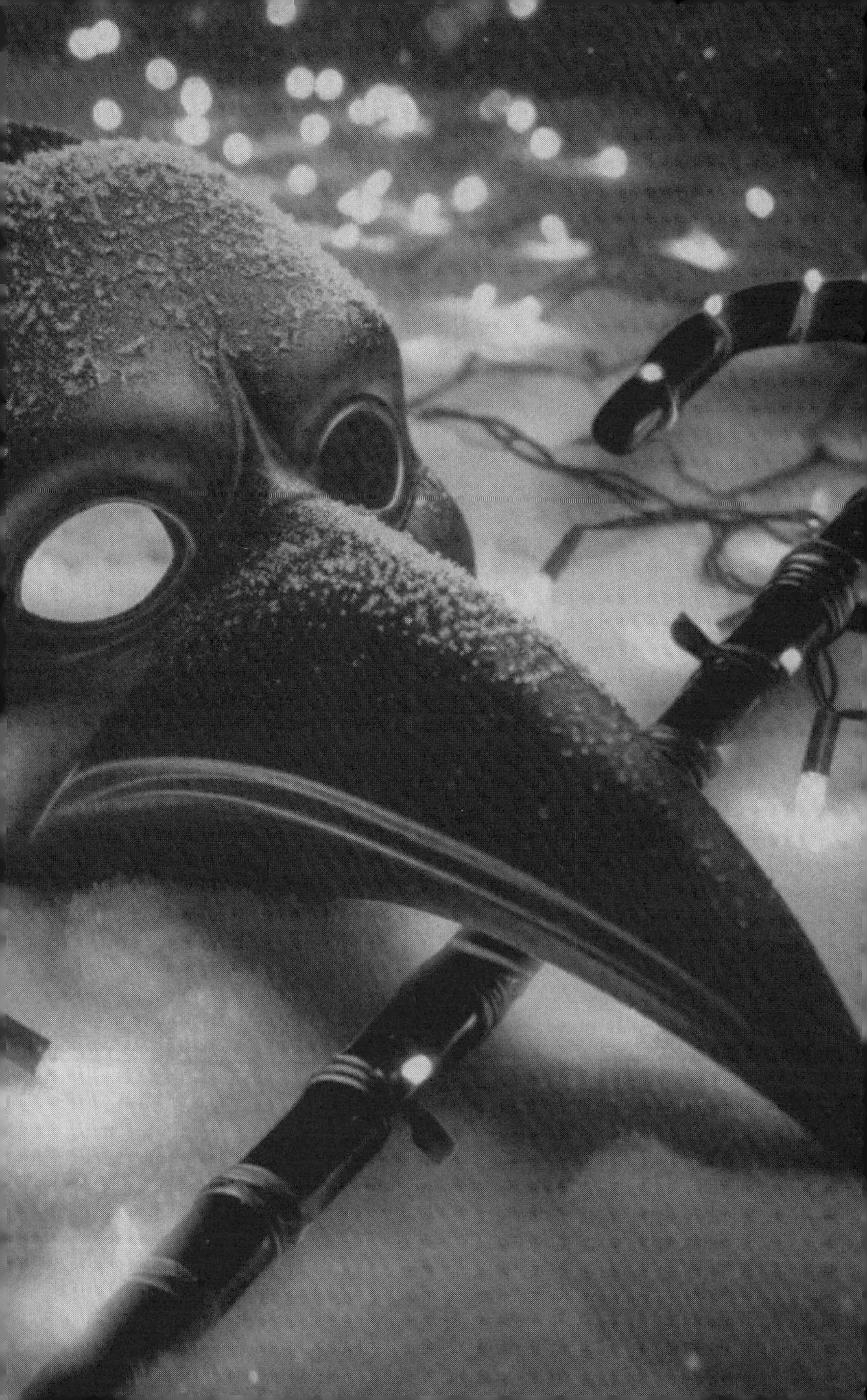

My breath catches, dread seeping into my veins.

"Didn't your daddy ever teach you not to talk to strangers?" he asks, his voice terrifyingly deep and distorted by what appears to be a voice changer.

I step back instinctively, my boots slipping slightly on the ice. My breathing quickens, each inhale sharper than the last as the primal sense of danger washes over me.

Something's wrong. Very fucking wrong.

The air changes and suddenly, he swivels, his movements fluid, and before I can react, he lunges. A scream tears from my throat as I spin on my heel, the snow bites at my legs. My boots try to gain grip as I run and aim for the woods, desperation and adrenaline propelling me forward.

Behind me, the crunch of snow grows louder. I dart through the trees that are layered in white, heart pounding, lungs burning, but no matter how fast I run, I feel him—closer with every step. A glance over my shoulder sends ice through my veins. He's still following, his stride measured, unhurried, like he's toying with me.

I veer sharply, pushing through the dense forest, branches clawing at my face and jacket. My sleeve catches on a thick branch, halting me with a sudden jolt. I wrench forward, hearing the fabric tear as my jacket is ripped from my body, leaving me in only my short dress. The cold bites instantly, seeping into my now bare skin.

"One, two, the plague is coming for you. Three, four, you better run, you whore," he sings from a short distance, the twisted melody echoing through the trees.

Suddenly, I hear something else—bells. Faint at first but growing louder. A jingle that doesn't belong here, doesn't belong anywhere, eerily harmonized with the rhythm of his footsteps.

Panic surges before my boots slip on the slick ground, and I stumble hard, crashing into the snow. Pain cuts through my knees as I claw at the icy ground, desperate to rise, but my limbs feel heavy, sluggish. I push myself up, my arms weak, snow clinging to my skin as the bells grow deafening.

Then it stops completely as his shadow looms over me, and I freeze, every nerve screaming.

The sharp jab of his cane prods my back, and I lurch forward, the icy ground rushing up to meet my face. Snow burns against my skin as I roll onto my back, gasping for air. He's there, towering above me, his breathless silence more oppressive than the cold.

The glowing cane presses against my throat and my chin lifts instinctively as the pressure cuts off my next breath.

"What do you want?" I whisper, the words trembling as they leave me, my chest rising and falling.

He tilts his head in response, the motion slow, calculated. Though the mask hides his expression, I can feel his eyes roaming over me, stripping me bare. The cane slides lower, deliberate and torturous, gliding down my neck and brushing between my breasts.

"Five, six, you're gonna take my dick," he murmurs, the eerie, distorted tune twisting into something vile and intimate. "Seven, eight, I know you cannot wait."

My pulse spikes as his words sink in, the horrifying truth of what he wants slamming into me. His cane moves further down, skimming my stomach before dipping toward my thighs.

I clamp my legs together, locking them tight against the invasive movement. His cane presses harder, insistent, but I refuse to spread them.

"You're fighting," he murmurs, the unrecognizable voice dripping with mockery. "But I've already won. Now show me what I'll be eating for Christmas dinner."

I shake my head once, my eyes wide, heart hammering so loudly it drowns out the world around me.

"Don't worry," he says, his voice calm but laced with malice. "It'll be our little secret. It always is. You don't want me to make you, do you?"

My brows pinch, the world around me tilting further. The seconds tick by, each heavier than the last, the reality of the situation tightening around me. I can't think. I can't fucking process.

"Open. Your. Fucking. Legs," he warns, his voice now sharp, each word slicing through the forest like a blade.

Instinct takes over, and without thinking, I twist onto my stomach, my body screaming to escape. I scramble onto all fours, but before I can move, he's on me.

A scream tears from my throat as his gloved hand tangles in my hair, yanking me back with brutal force. The sound echoes through the area and he drops onto his knees behind me, dragging me back until I'm forced onto my knees between his thighs. My back slams into his chest, feeling the hard edges of his body.

103

The cane slides over the front of my throat, locking into place, and my head is forced back onto his shoulder. I clutch at the cane, my fingers clawing at it desperately, trying to stop the choking hold.

From the corner of my eye, I glimpse the beak of his mask, its shadowed eyes hollow, inhuman. His breath, harsh and ragged, echoes in my ear, mirroring my frantic gasps.

The danger is no longer a threat—it's here, pressing into me, surrounding around me. His gaze drops to my chest, and though I can't see his eyes, I feel the weight of it like a brand.

"I don't want to just hurt you, snowflake," he growls, the threat wrapped in a warped, almost personal tone. "I want to play with you while I'm doing it."

"Doing what?" I gasp.

He doesn't answer right away, the pause more horrifying than any words. The hunter in him enjoys the moment, savoring my fear like its fuel. He growls before removing the flashing cane, tosses it into the snow in front of us, but his gloved hand replaces it, wrapping tightly around my throat, keeping my head back against him.

His other hand presses down into the front of my dress, and my body tightens instantly. My hands shoot up to grab his wrist, preparing to scream from the assault. But when he grabs my breast, the grip is all too familiar—despite the gloves—and a whimper slips from my throat before I can stop it.

He toys with my nipple, pinching it between his fingers, and my back arches, the pain a cruel mix of pleasure and torment.

"Nine, ten, I'm gonna make you come again." His voice is a low sneer in my ear, and my eyes flutter shut as my body betrays me, responding to the command.

"Rook…" I whisper, my voice broken. "What are you—"

I try to tug on his arm again, but his grip around my throat tightens, cutting off my words.

"Obedience isn't an option, little sister.. It's the only way you're gonna survive me this Christmas."

I can't respond. The cold, the fear, the sinful pleasure—it all merges into something I can't escape. His hand remains tight around my throat, suffocating the air from my lungs, while his other rips from my breast and moves between my legs from behind.

"Mine to break. Mine to shape. Mine to keep, with no escape."

The sudden intrusion of his gloved fingers moving over my pussy has me gasping, my thighs clenching instinctively, but he doesn't relent. He shoves them inside my hole with one hard, brutal plunge. I scream, my eyes snapping wide open, my back arching, but he only drives him further, opening me up. The leather fabric rams into me relentlessly and repeatedly, fucking me hard, each thrust a cruel reminder of how helpless I am.

His hand slides from my throat to my mouth, muffling my cries, the leather of his glove pressing against my lips. He fingerbangs me hard, the violent stretch forcing my body to double cross me. My climax builds fast, too fast, but just as I near the edge, he tears his fingers away in a single cruel motion. My body aches, throbbing with need, trembling from the sudden, hollow ache he's left behind.

I hear it before I feel it: the metallic clink of his belt unbuckling, the sound loud in the frigid air. He works quickly, hungrily, his breath heavy in my ear, every exhale filled with urgency. When he reaches into his boxers, freeing himself, the cold doesn't seem to bother him—it's nothing compared to the heat radiating off his body, the way he presses the pierced tip of his cock against my entrance.

"Sink that perfect cunt onto me," he growls, his voice thick with need.

I don't refuse. I never do when it comes to Rook. My body responds before my mind can resist, and I begin to take him in. Inch by inch, it feels too much after so long, his piercing scraping along my walls, but I keep going, my nails digging into his arm for balance.

With a savage motion, he grabs the hem of my dress, yanking it up and bunching it at my waist before pulling the neckline down hard enough to tear. My breasts bounce free, bare to the icy air as my brows knit together, fighting to take him deeper.

When I'm fully seated, my pussy completely full of his thick dick, the sensation sends a violent shudder through me. Rook doesn't wait any longer. He grabs my breast roughly, his thumb grazing over my nipple as he squeezes hard enough to bruise, and the pain sends a rush of something dark and wicked coursing through me.

My hips begin to move, sliding up his length, leaving a trail of wetness in my wake until I feel the edge of him, then plunge back down.

I moan loudly, my voice a broken, desperate sound as I take him again and again, each thrust erasing the world around me, addicted to the feel of him. It doesn't matter that I could be getting frostbite, or that I'm riding my big brother's cock in the snowy woods on Christmas Eve. All that matters is the way he fills me, the way he consumes me, the way I keep coming back for more.

As my thrusts grow aggressive, my pussy slamming down on him with desperate rhythm, Rook suddenly shoves me forward, the motion so forceful I nearly fall face-first into the snow. My hands sink into the icy ground to steady myself, his cane casting flickering light over my body from underneath and my tits dangle freely, swaying with every panting breath.

He positions himself behind me, his grip on my waist like iron as he yanks me backward, arching my spine to his liking. When he eases his pants further down, I know there will be no mercy—only more length of his big dick and more of his pent-up hunger.

He doesn't wait. There's no hesitation, no compassion as I thought. He drags his cock back, before slamming it back inside me with such force that I cry out. His feral snarl reverberates through the forest at the same time as my shameful scream.

The pounding is ruthless, each drive deeper, harder, tearing into the core of me. My body trembles, every part of me pushed to my limit as he claims me again and again. My tits jump wildly from the power, my nipples grazing over the snow as if it's a reminder of the icy world outside the molten chaos we're creating. The heat between us burns hotter, wetter—I can feel it dripping down my thighs.

"Rook!" I scream, hoping to slow his pace, but he simply reaches over, his hand tangling in my hair with a savage yank that snaps my head back. I yelp but my pain only fuels his pleasure.

"Stay the fuck still and take it," he scowls, his other hand pressing firmly on the middle of my back, bending me further, locking me in place as he smashes his cock into me with a vicious purpose. It's almost unbearable, but my body seems to give itself over completely.

My legs shake violently with the strain, while my freezing fingers dig into the snow, curling into tight fists. Not able to hold any longer, my body explodes, shattering into a million pieces. Ecstasy crashes through me, and a cry tears from my throat.

Even as I spasm uncontrollably, my pussy clenching tight around his cock, Rook doesn't slow down. No, he pushes through my intense orgasm, his rhythm sending me spiraling into another world entirely.

My vision blurs, the edges warping as the overstimulation devours me. The ground feels unsteady, the woods whirling, and I'm on the verge of collapse. But then, I feel it.

He presses deep, burying himself completely, and his cock swells, widening me further as a flood of heat surges inside me. His thick cum fills me, each hot pump pushing me closer to the periphery of a blackout.

A low, guttural growl escapes him, his body swaying from the force of release. His grip loosens suddenly, his fingers untangling from my hair, and I fall forward, tumbling into the ground, exhausted.

His cock slides out of my battered, cum-filled pussy, leaving me open and sore. I lie there, chest heaving, the snow beneath me melting. Even with my eyes closed, I can feel his green orbs observing, probably satisfied with the way he just ruined me. I hear his zipper pull up and then the fastening of his belt. Just when I think he's done with me and will take me home now, he does the opposite.

He stands, looming over me and sneaks his arm around the middle of my body. With little effort, he lifts my deadweight and slings me over his shoulder like I weigh nothing to him.

As he walks with me, my daze eyes open, and all I see is my long-wet hair swaying, his boots crunching over the snow and his lit-up cane. His arm strengthens around the back of my thighs for a second before his hand takes full advantage of the moment, grabbing my bare ass cheek before he delivers a sharp smack. I squeak, my body jerking, and he chuckles lowly.

Just when I'm about to ask him where the hell he's taking me, I lift my head. I glance around, noticing it's just woodland, no car in sight, not road and I'm confused, but my confusion is short lived as I suddenly hear metal doors opening.

He climbs inside the vehicle, and I am lowered onto what appears to be fur. As I look up, I see him hovering over me, the plague mask still intact, but it's what's behind him that catches my attention. Christmas lights twinkle against chains on the ceiling of what appears to be a transit van, a simple mistletoe hanging in the middle. My brows pinch as I start to look around frantically. Tinted windows, fur blankets beneath me, a turned off heater.

"What the fuck, Rook?" I gasp, as I meet his black, hollowed eyes. "What is this?"

His head tilts slightly, the motion almost mocking. "It's where we'll be spending the night," he responds, his voice calm but strange through the mask. "Together."

He glances around, admiring his work like a disturbed artist admiring his masterpiece and his next words drip with menace.

"Within the cold walls of this metal shell, bunny, there will be no silent night tonight—only an unholy night."

My chest tightens, my breath quickening as I shake my head, trying to reason with him. "But Dad, he'll—"

His warning growl slices through my protest as his eyes flash to mine. "Here we fucking go," he sneers, his tone drenched in scorn. "Ebony has the rare opportunity to spend Christmas alone with her brother, and she's too wrapped up in daddy's chains to be a woman and make her own fucking decisions."

The fury in his words ignites a spark of rage in me, and my eyes squint, the tension crackling between us. "But little does she know..." His masked face dips lower, the sharp tip of the beak pressing against my lips. "She has no choice. My sister is mine tonight. All. Mine. All. Fucking. Night. And she will be an obedient little slut for me."

I shake my head once, defiance building in my chest, but he doesn't want to hear it. Without a word, he withdraws, slipping out of the van. I sit up quickly, my breath hitching as the doors slam behind him, the click of the lock sealing me inside.

Through the tinted window, I watch as he stalks around to the front, his dark silhouette moving through the snowfall. My gaze shifts, and I realize the front of the van is blocked off completely.

A low snarl escapes me, frustration mounting, until the engine roars to life. The van lurches forward, and I steady myself, my eyes darting to the chains and Christmas lights swaying ominously above me.

What the fuck is this?

I yank my dress down over my legs and tug the fabric up to cover my exposed tits, my heart hammering as I scramble to my knees, desperate to see where he's taking me.

The landscape rushes past until, suddenly, the frozen expanse of a lake comes into view. My heart stutters, cold dread gripping me tight. Memories attack my mind of the Christmas I fell into one. The icy water swallowing me whole, my lungs burning, my frantic struggles to find a way out. I almost drowned that day, saved at the last possible moment. And Rook... he's never forgiven himself for not being the one to pull me out.

The van jerks to a stop, reversing until the back rests dangerously close to the lake's edge. I don't need to ask what he's fucking doing—I know his game. Asshole. He thinks this will trap me, that fear will keep me confined.

Yeah, we'll see about that.

The engine cuts off, plunging the van into silence. I rise to my feet, my body hunched beneath the low roof, every muscle coiled as I watch him approach the back doors. My pulse thunders as I see his shadow moving closer, and the second he swings the doors open, I lunge forward with a scream, slamming into him with all my weight.

He grunts as his boots skid on the ice, the momentum sending him crashing backward with a hard thud. I land on top of him, the ice beneath us cracking dangerously.

I laugh breathlessly, excitement and fear mixing as I prepare to crawl off him, but his hands clamp down on my waist, making me immobile.

"Let me go, asshole!" I thrash against his grip, kicking and twisting, but he's far too strong as always.

His arms tighten around my back like steel bands, and with a low, dark snicker, he begins to rise, lifting me.

"You ain't escaping that easily, bunny," he taunts, his voice laced with wicked amusement.

I go insane, my body fighting as I scream, but he doesn't give a shit. Without a care, he climbs back into the van and forces me inside with him.

I land on my knees and before I can do anything else, he yanks a chain down from the ceiling. The metal clinks and rattles as my arms are wrenched upward, the freezing links locking around my wrists, suspending me in place.

I'm trapped.

My chest heaves with panicked breaths, but he doesn't stop there. As if to strip away any last shred of dignity, he grabs the fabric of my dress and, in one brutal motion, rips it from my body. Then grabs Blaise's hairclip and tears it from my scalp, tossing it aside.

I gasp, the shock of the sudden exposure sending a wave of humiliation crashing over me. Naked, I sit there, vulnerable and bound, every inch of me laid bare under his ruthless gaze. His hand suddenly grips my face, his fingers cruelly pinching my cheeks, forcing my lips into a tight line.

"Fucking stop it." His voice is a low growl, filled with warning and threat. He releases my face with a sharp shove, pushing my head to the side.

I shake my head, trying to move the strands of hair from my eyes. I watch, helpless, as he removes his leather jacket, the material sliding off his shoulders with ease. He's shirtless now, his tatted skin rippling under the dim light of the van. My chest tightens as my gaze unwillingly traces over his muscular body; my breath lodged in my throat.

I close my thighs as soon as I feel his cum starting to leak out of me and sit back on my knees and he leans back against the cold, metal shell of the van, one knee bent lazily, the other leg stretched out in front of him.

His posture is relaxed, almost as if he's enjoying the moment, watching me struggle beneath his control. The doors of the van hang wide open, the freezing cold air pouring in and seeps into my bones. I feel my nipples harden, my lips turning an angry shade of blue.

The silence draws out as he stares at me from behind that mask and I stare back.

"What's with the mask? Why are you doing this?"

He thinks about my question for a moment, then responds calmly.

"Remember when you called me The Plague last time I saw you two years ago, bunny? Said I was nothing but a fucking disease that infects everything I touch—even your soul?" He breathes against the cold air before continuing, "Yeah... I remember too. But now I'm back to finish what I started. Consequences be damned."

I swallow, feeling my body fall with defeat, that night coming back at me all at once.

CHAPTER NINE

- FLASHBACK -

ROOK

My gaze locks onto Ebony, curled up against the headboard, her naked body shaking, her bright blue eyes drowning in fear and tears. The Christmas lights still bind her wrists, cutting into her pale skin, a cruel misrepresentation of innocence.

She's trapped, helpless. A fragile bird in the jaws of a captor. Me.

"You think you can just fuck my daughter? Your SISTER! In MY house?" Ryker's roar splits the suffocating silence, his voice a feral snarl that reverberates through the room.

His body tenses, a fighter ready to pounce, every tendon of his frame screaming violence. But I don't back down, I never do. I meet his rage with a cold stare, raising an eyebrow as if he's nothing more than an irritation. Because he fucking is.

"I didn't just fuck her," I growl. "I destroyed her—for any other pathetic excuse of a fucking man you'd try to sell her off to."

His fists clench, his face twisting with fury and he takes a step toward me, but then he freezes when he hears her.

"Daddy don't!" Ebony screams, her voice breaking like glass.

His chest heaves, but his anger doesn't ease. Instead, he spins on his heel, his eyes locking onto her naked form.

"You're a disgrace!" he bellows, the harshness in his words enough to make her shrink into herself. She cowers under his disgust, her fear filling the room and it pisses me the fuck off.

But when he raises his hand, his intention to hit her obvious, something inside me snaps. I don't think—I just act. I lunge forward, my fist flying, and I drive a hard blow into his ribs from behind. The satisfying crunch of impact makes him groan, his body buckling.

But it's not enough. As I pull back to strike again, he recovers, spinning and his fist collides with my jaw, pain exploding through my skull. I stagger back, spitting blood, but before I can regain my footing, he charges, slamming his shoulder into my stomach. The impact drives me into the cupboard, the power shattering glass and wood, sending shards raining around us.

Pain flares, but the wrath and resentment only fuel me. I slam my elbow down, once, twice, again and again, smashing into the back of his head and neck with bone-crunching force. The world narrows, everything reduced to the raw heat of violence and hate I have for him. Ebony's screams pierce the haze, but they feel distant. All I see is red and murder. I can't—and won't—fucking stop.

He lunges for my throat, fingers outstretched like claws, but I move back just in time. My fist swings again, colliding with his nose with a crack. Blood spurts, but Ryker doesn't waver. The bastard is like steel—ruthless even when he's calm, and now, his fucking rage makes him unstoppable.

We tear into each other, fists flying, bodies colliding in a chaos of violence and every punch lands like a thunderclap. The room is a mess, smashed to pieces, the sound of hard blows and ragged grunts filling the air.

"Stop it! Both of you, stop!" My mom's scream cuts through the noise as she frantically rushes into the room.

She tries to wedge herself between us, but we're past the point of reason. The anger is too raw, all too consuming, too much hatred between us and we keep ripping chunks out of one another like animals in a cage fight.

Then Ryker does what he always does—escalates. His hand shoots to the back of his jeans, and he yanks out his gun.

The air freezes. Time itself seems to stop.

As he levels the barrel at my forehead, my mom's shaky breath hitches, and Ebony whimpers, curling tighter into herself like she could disappear. I meet his gaze head on with an expression as calm as death, my chin raised.

"Please, Ryker…" My mom begs in a whisper.

Blood pours from his broken nose, his eyes wild, barely human. I've always known it would end like this, with a gun in his hand because that's the type of coward he is.

"I love her," I say, my tone even, unshaken. "I always have and I always fucking will."

Ryker laughs—a cold sound that's more disbelief than humor. He cocks the gun with a click, the metallic sound making Ebony scream. She buries her face in her thighs again, shaking, unable to bear the sight of what's coming.

"Fucking love her?" he spits, his teeth stained red, his fury boiling over. He takes a step closer, pressing the barrel harder against my skull. "You know she's your little sister, right?"

His voice is full of disgust as he continues. "No," he snarls, his lips curling in a sneer. "You didn't love her, Rook. You fucking used her. Used her to get to me. One last shot from your cunt father to worm under my skin."

My jaw tightens at his accusation. Of course, Ryker would twist this into something like that—it's all he knows. His history with my dad has poisoned his every thought, and how he treats me has always shown that, but he couldn't be more wrong with this one. I didn't fucking choose this.

I didn't want to fall for the enemy's daughter, my stepsister. But here I am—weakly, irreversibly and utterly in love with her.

I couldn't give a flying fuck about the hatred between our dads. It doesn't even cross my mind when it comes to her. She's not her father's shadow, nor the reflection of what he is. She's his opposite, a flicker of warmth in a winter that seeks to freeze me whole.

And maybe that's why she means so much to me. She's the one thing in my life that feels steady, even when everything else is shaking. As long as I have Ebony, I have a fucking reason—something to hold on to when the rest of the world slips through my fingers.

"No, he wouldn't," my mom tries to protest.

"Shut the fuck up, Cindy!" he growls, and his tone with her ignites something primal in me and I see lose it.

"Don't talk to my mom like that, you cunt!" I snarl, stepping forward, my fists curling.

His response is immediate and brutal. The gun lifts, and before I can react, the butt slams into my face. Pain explodes as blood gushes from my nose. I groan, my hand flying to my face in an attempt to stop the bleeding.

"Fucking pussy, as always," I sneer. "Weapons. Weapons. Weapons. That's all you've got." I lower my hand, my glare deathly. "Fight me like a man!" I bark, my body vibrating with fury.

He steps closer, so close our bodies brush, and his eyes are harsh, unblinking, searching mine with a manic intensity.

"You're way over your head, kid," he says and his teeth clench so hard I can hear them grind. "You leave tonight."

My brows furrow and I feel Ebony's gaze from across the room, but Ryker continues, his words hitting like bullets.

"You're not being around my daughter. You're done here." His tone is final.

He gestures with the barrel of the gun, a commanding motion toward the door. "Go get your shit. Don't make me put a bullet between your eyes."

I glance at Ebony, and the sight of her guts me. She's staring at me, wide-eyed as tears stream down her face, and she mouths the words I don't want to hear.

Just do it.

My teeth clench so hard my jaw aches, and the fire in my chest burns out, leaving only ashes and defeat. Slowly, I turn around while hearing my mom rushing toward Ebony, her voice shaky as she works to untie her, whispering something too low for me to hear.

Ryker's heavy steps follow me like a shadow as I make my way to the guest room where my bags are and when I enter, I reach for one, collecting my stuff. For a moment, Ryker stands in the doorway, watching me like a killer sizing up his target.

Then, without warning, he steps back, slamming the door shut behind him. The click of the lock echoes through the room, sealing me in.

I rush toward it, my heart racing, dread tightening around my chest. The thought of him hurting Ebony hits me and I grab the handle, yanking it repeatedly, but the door doesn't budge. My breathing grows shallow as I slam my fist against the wood in frustration. Finally, I press my ear to it, listening for any sound.

Muffled voices reach my ear from down the hallway. Nothing clear, but there's no sign of a struggle, no screams from my mom. She would be screaming by now if he was hurting her. I exhale a deep breath before moving to the bed and sit on the edge, lowering my head into my hands.

My mind races and minutes crawl to what feels like hours until finally, the lock clicks. I shoot to my feet as the door opens slowly, but it's Ebony who steps inside, her head down, her frame small and defeated in the oversized shirt she's wearing. Relief floods through me while she closes the door softly behind her and lifts her head, her red eyes meeting mine.

No emotion. Just hollow.

I step forward but stop when I notice the way she holds herself, stiff and wary. She pauses, and for a moment, we're both frozen. Then I move again, gently grabbing her wrist and pulling her toward me. My hands find her face, tilting her chin up, and her watery eyes meet mine. Her body is limp in my hands, like the fight has drained out of her completely.

"Leave with me," I whisper, searching her gaze, desperate for the spark I know is still in there somewhere. "Just me and you. We can get out of here. Start over somewhere else—somewhere where none of this fucking bullshit can touch us."

She blinks at me, her expression unreadable, and I tighten my grip on her face, wanting her to listen. "You're the only thing that matters to me," I say, my voice breaking as I lean closer.

Her lips tremble, and tears begin to fall again, her hands wrapping around my wrists.

"Please…" she whispers, shaking her head slightly and her eyes close, more tears streaming down her cheeks. "I can't."

Her words hit me like a punch to the gut, but I shake her gently, forcing her eyes back to mine. "Yes, you fucking can," I snap, my voice rising. "Don't you love me?"

A sob escapes her, loud and raw, but she doesn't answer. For a long moment, her silence cuts deeper than anything she could say. Then, she shakes her head once—just once—and my world shatters.

"No. Not like that."

The words are quiet but final, and they tear through me causing my hands drop away. I step back, turning away from her as my vision blurs. My chest aches, and I rub my hand across my mouth, closing my eyes tightly, trying to stop the tears stinging my eyes.

"I'm sorry, Rook," she croaks.

I shake my head. She's fucking lying. She has to be lying. I feel it every second I'm with her. It's not fake. I turn back to her, my steps quick and my hands slamming against the door on either side of her, caging her in.

"You're fucking lying, Bunny," I growl, a tear slipping down my cheek. "Why do you keep lying about it?"

Her head snaps up, and her blue eyes blaze with anger—real, burning anger.

"I'm not lying, Rook!" she shouts, her voice cracking with emotion. "I've been telling you for months to leave me the fuck alone. And now look at what we've done! My dad saw me naked! He caught me being fucked by my own brother on Christmas Eve, and all you can think about is this—about whisking me off like some fairytale ending that doesn't fucking exist!"

"I feel it, Bunny. I see it every damn day. You can pretend all you want to everyone else, like a little fucking coward, but at least I have the guts to admit what I want. YOU."

She sucks in a sharp breath, but her glare doesn't waver, then she explodes.

"Why do you always have to do this? Huh?! Why can't you just accept it? I don't want you! I've told you over and over, Rook—I DON'T FUCKING WANT YOU!"

Her words slice sharper than a knife and my teeth grind, my whole-body trembling violently as more tears stream down my face. Everything she says is poison, seeping into me, eating me the fuck alive.

"You're like the plague," she hisses, her eyes blazing with fury and disgust. "You infect everything you touch—even my fucking soul. You can't take no for an answer, can you? You had to tear our family apart. You're always smothering me. Corrupting me. Breaking down every part of me. Touching me. Pushing me. I can't breathe around you, Rook! Why the fuck would I want to be with you?"

I press my fists against the door, my knuckles white, my breaths coming fast and sharp as her words slice through me, but I don't stop her. I take every hit, every stab to the heart like a fool.

"You wanted to fuck me?!" she hisses. "Well, you got what you wanted! Mission fucking accomplished. You broke me down! You won!"

My bruised face twists, the pain of her accusation too much to hold back. "You think that's all it was? A fucking game?" I ask, every word spiked with confusion and anger. "Why the fuck would I put myself through this—through all this… suffering— just for a body? Yeah, I say fucked-up shit. I do fucked-up shit. A brother shouldn't say or do half the things I've done to you. But one thing has been real through all of it is, I fucking love you, Ebony. You could've had that pussy sewn up, locked away, and I'd still choose you. I chase and continue to chase like a weak ass little bitch because I still cling to hope that one day maybe, just maybe, you'd choose me!"

Her scoff cuts through me like a whip and she looks away, disdain written all over her face. "Well, get over it," she says coldly. "I'm not interested in having a relationship with my brother."

Something in me snaps and I slam my palms against the hard door by either side of her head, the sound echoing like a gunshot.

My body shakes as a roar rips from my chest, so real and pained filled, it rattles through the room, every ounce of misery I've kept hidden, unleashed, right in front of her face.

Her body jerks in shock, stiffening, her wide eyes staring into mine as tears flood down my cheeks. My breathing is uneven, my chest heaving as I stagger back.

"YOU'RE FUCKING EVERYTHING TO ME! YOU'RE ALL I THINK ABOUT... ALL I FUCKING WANT!" I scream at the top of my lungs.

"AND YOU CAN'T HAVE ME!" she yells back, her body vibrating, her wet eyes blazing, then she points her finger at me, dropping her tone. "You need to leave me the fuck alone!"

My face suddenly falls. "Fuck you, Ebony," I whisper, the words flat and lifeless.

My emotions now feel dead as I search her gaze one last time, desperately looking for something, anything—but when I finally see there's nothing left, I turn my back on her.

The silence between us is deafening until I hear her take a careful step toward me and her hand brushes against mine.

"Rook…" she whispers, her voice soft, almost pleading.

I pull away, jerking my hand from hers like her touch burns.

"Don't," I mutter, shaking my head from side to side, my voice hoarse and broken. I sniff, my chest tightening with downfall as I wipe my tear-streaked face with my hand. I'm just fucking done.

"Just get the fuck out," I rasp, low and final, hardly able to breath.

CHAPTER TEN

- PRESENT -

Ebony

I stare at him, panting as that night crashes over me like a tidal wave, guilt clawing at my insides. My eyes streak with tears as I swallow the lump rising in my throat.

"What's wrong, Ebony?" he says blankly, "Remember how you tore my heart fucking out and stamped all over it?"

I blink in a daze as he points to his mask, tapping the beak. "You created this. This fucking monster inside me. And I'm gonna make sure you never forget it. I'm the plague doctor, infected with a sickness and tonight, you're my only cure."

Before I can even process what he just said, he moves, grabbing something from the side of him, and when I see the black tape in his hands, a chill runs down my spine. My heart skips a beat, and I try to take a breath, but it's like the air has been sucked out of the van. Then he's already on his knees in front of me, tearing the tape with a harsh, ripping sound.

"Rook, I—"

The words die in my throat as the cold tape is slapped over my mouth, silencing me.

"Shut the fuck up. Your disobedience is annoying."

He searches my watery eyes before leaning in and flattening his tongue against my cheek, slowly dragging it upward with a growl, collecting every tear and ounce of the pain he's causing.

"I'm going to screw every part of you so fucking hard this Christmas, Bunny. By the time I've finished toying with you, your name will be nothing but a forgotten whisper, like a shitty stain erased from my crazed mind forever. I'll be rid of you, sis," he murmurs, his tone cracking just enough to show he's losing his sanity. "Whether you'll be able to scrub me off your skin, feel anything but me crawling beneath it for the rest of your miserable life afterward—is your fucking problem."

I almost roll my eyes, defiance swirling inside me before I watch and listen to him move behind me, the sound of fabric rustling, and my pulse quickens.

"I feel like my little sister needs to be taught a lesson or two. She clearly thinks she can cock tease her big brother for years and there won't be any repercussions."

When I glance down, I see him holding something—a piece of black lingerie, delicate and sheer. The thin fabric barely covers my nipples as he slides it over my breasts. My body jerks, the heat of the moment coursing through me, but I don't get the chance to react before he ties the thin strings at my back.

"She's going to do as she's told. No buts, no ifs, no fucking nos. She'll surrender and obey. And only then, maybe... maybe I'll think about letting her go."

The words hang in the air, as if I'm not even here—like I'm some fucking item dangling from the ceiling. I bite back the urge to snap at him because obviously I can't. But it's clear now. He's made his intentions so fucking obvious. This Christmas isn't about a lovely reunion, or anything close to it. It's about power, revenge, and getting under my skin until there's nothing left but raw, desperate surrender. That's what he always wants.

The thing is... after the shit I've been through tonight, and for the past two years, I'm not sure I care anymore. Maybe, just maybe, I'll let him wreck me. Because the truth is, I don't even know what the fuck I want any more or where my life is heading for that matter. All I know is, being here with him, I'm strangely safe, even if he plans to screw the life out of me, I'm going to secretly enjoy every damn second of this.

Next, his hands are on my hips, sliding a matching pair of panties up my legs. I can't help but tense as they wedge far up my ass crack before he ties them into bows high on my hips, emphasizing every curve.

He knows what he's doing. He's clearly thought about this more than fucking once. Creep.

And then I hear it—soft jingling bells. His fingers gently graze my neck, moving my hair aside before he brings a black collar in front of me, the row of silver bells on it tinkling in the quiet. The cool leather rests against my skin, and I gulp as he whispers against my ear.

"Just in case you try to escape me again... I'll fucking find you. You won't be able to hide from me with this beauty around your throat."

The click of the buckle reaches my ears, and my throat tightens as he fastens it behind me, locking it in place. But despite everything, a needy little shudder runs through me.

My pussy is already betraying me.

"Then there's this..." He lifts something into view in front of me, and my eyes widen. His low chuckle vibrates against my ear, muffled by the mask obscuring his face.

"Do you know what it is, bunny?" His tone is a taunt, thick with sadistic amusement.

I stay silent because I have no choice, but yeah, I know what the hell it is.

"Of course you do," he sneers. "My little sister is an anal slut, after all." The words pierce me, equal parts shame and heat blooming inside as he continues. "But don't worry. Naughty girls always get plenty of dick in their ass at Christmas. And I can't fucking wait to give you plenty of mine."

I fixate on the glossy, black butt plug poised between his tattooed fingers, shining against the twinkling lights hanging above. A white, fluffy bunny tail is attached to it—a cruel joke that doesn't escape me.

"An hour with this buried inside your asshole while your cunt is fucked, filled, and ruined, and I'll slide right in," he says gravelly, voice dripping with filth.

His disgusting words send my mind reeling. Every syllable, every depraved threat, undoes me more. He's mad—unhinged in ways I can't fully understand—but God help me, I crave his degradation.

Still, I can't help but wonder: how far does his depravity go? How much darker can this Christmas night fall? I guess I'm about to find out.

CHAPTER ELEVEN

ROOK

I stare down at her perfect, peachy ass, my thoughts coiling tighter with wicked plans. Dark fantasies pulse through me, daring me to push her further, to see how completely I can shatter her tonight.

No one can hear her—not her gasps, not her fucking screams. It's just the two of us and this Christmas night that feels stolen, drenched in sin.

After lowering the butt plug between her legs and placing it on the fur blanket, my palm glides over the curve of her smooth ass, firm and possessive. I squeeze her juicy flesh, hard enough to leave angry marks, and she flinches—her body deceiving her as arches into me. Hooking my finger beneath the delicate string of her panties wedged tightly between her cheeks, I pull it aside with aching slowness, exposing both her holes to me.

Shifting closer, I press my groin against her, her bare skin flush against the rough denim of my jeans. My cock is already hard, leaking, throbbing against her, eager for relief, but I'm gonna play first. My hand slides lower, slipping between her thighs from behind, while my other hand trails up the front of her stomach, feeling the shivers scattering over her cold skin.

When my finger's part her slick pussy lips, she sucks in a sharp breath. I explore her slowly, but roughly, rubbing her wetness across her swollen clit, coaxing it to ache under my touch. My fingers tease deeper, slick with her arousal, circling her entrance before gliding inside her cunt.

She clenches around me, her thighs tensing as I enter her, pushing further. My other hand sneaks under her bra, the thin lace no match for the greedy grip I take on her breast. Her nipple hardens beneath my palm as I squeeze, vicious enough to draw a gasp.

My fingers in her pussy move excruciatingly slow against her silky walls in a rhythm intended to push her right to the edge and hold her there. Her legs start to give out, the tension in her body unbearable. She wants to fall, but she can't, not with me here and the chains keeping her swinging. She's forced to suffer. Caught between what she wants and what I won't fucking give.

Then my fingers shift, dragging out and skimming higher, firmly circling the tight rim of her asshole. She stiffens instantly, her breath catching in her throat as I press against it.

My hand leaves her tit, moving upward to wrap around the front of her throat. I grip it fiercely, my fingers pressing into her delicate skin—a silent warning to take it. Her pulse beats frantically against my palm as I force her head back.

I ease my wet fingers into her puckered ring. Her body fights the intrusion, the tightness making it nearly impossible to breach her. But I don't stop. I press harder, until I slide past the barrier and into her, feeling the smooth heat of her forbidden walls around my digits as they force her to accept me.

Knuckle deep, I pause, then I pull my fingers out, before thrusting them back in. Her reaction is immediate—a low, breathy moan slipping against the tape.

"Good girl," I growl into her ear, my voice rough with approval.

Her body is mine, every fucking inch of it, and her ass feels so good—just like everything else she has to offer.

I work my fingers deeper, curling and twisting, pushing her past the limits of her control, demanding her muscles yield. The fight fuels me, makes me more aggressive, the sadistic edge in my mind slipping into overdrive as I stretch and violate her, forcing her to loosen up for me. She pulses around me, her body deceiving her almost right away as she climax's without warning. Her come spills down her inner thighs, glistening in the low light.

I pull my fingers free, smearing the wetness over her swollen pussy before shoving them back inside her ass again. The way her hole clenches, then gives way, drives me fucking mad with the power I hold over her. Her muffled screams tear through the air as I finger bang her, raw and desperate, but there's no hesitation in her body.

She's perfect like this and I can't get enough. Never get enough.

Reaching up, I unlock the chains binding her wrists and the moment her arms are free, she collapses forward, her hands bracing against the fur floor to catch herself.

I grunt, shoving her down with a firm press of my palm on her back and her head dips low, her ass lifting high into the air, entirely vulnerable to do what the fuck I want. My fingers remain embedded inside her, her muscles flutter around me and I growl.

"Stay the fuck there," I order. "Let's see how wide I can get this asshole of yours."

My eyes sweep over her, following the sharp curve of her back until they land on my fingers in her ruined little hole.

I use my knees to push her legs even wider, forcing her to spread for me. My free hand reaches for the plague mask still covering my face. The leather straps bite into my skin as I rip it off, tossing it carelessly to the floor.

I don't need it right now. That comes later.

My tongue slides over two fingers from my free hand, coating them with saliva, before bringing them to her asshole as well. My other hand remains steady, fingers already deep inside her, pressing against her tight walls while I add the new fingers, the struggle is harsh and thrilling as I ease them in alongside the others.

Her body strains, muscles taut with the effort of trying to handle what I'm putting her through. My eyes flicker to her side profile, partly hidden by the curtain of her shiny black hair. Her eyes are shut tight, her breath coming in shallow gasps. Her hands claw at the fur beneath her, fingers curling into it like it's the only thing keeping her together.

When all four fingers are fully in her, my movements slow, testing her. I work her inch by inch, dragging all my fingers up and down her walls for some time until I begin to pull and press at the same time, making her spread with each drive. Her asshole spasms, but I don't stop, the battle only fueling the warped pleasure building inside me.

A low, guttural growl escapes my lips as I lean forward, gathering spit on my tongue. I let it fall in a glistening strand, aimed perfectly, and I watch it disappear inside the pink void. Again and again, I repeat the sickening process—spitting, fingering, stretching her ruthlessly.

She doesn't stop me. She fucking can't. I'm breaking her in the most callous way my fucked-up mind could conjure, and fuck, I love every second of it. Her submission, the way her body gives way to me, feeds the madness inside me like nothing else ever could.

Slowly, I ease my fingers out of her, her body shuddering as I do. My hands clamp down on her ass cheeks, squeezing hard enough to leave marks, my jaw tightening with dark satisfaction. Without warning, I lift one hand and bring it down in a sharp, stinging slap against her fatty flesh. The crack of it echoes, her scream splitting the silence as my palm leaves my vivid, red imprint on her skin.

Spreading her cheeks wide, I lean in, my tongue darting out and sliding into her still-gaping asshole. The warmth of her makes my head spin, and I press deeper, licking, tasting her walls, owning her in a way that's purely natural. Her gasp is loud, and her hand shoots back, fingers tangling in my hair as if forcing me to continue.

But I'm harsh. I fuck her as far as I can with my tongue, my lips pressing and sucking around the pink ring, my teeth grazing just enough to make her whimper. Her moans build, louder, more frantic, as I ravage her without a shred of mercy. My grip on her tightens, spreading her open further, leaving her no room to escape the onslaught.

I lift her cheeks higher, dripping lower until I'm at her weeping pussy. My thumb's part her puffy lips, and I plunge in, tongue slipping through her folds, flicking her clit before sliding back up. She's shuddering now as I devour her, her thighs quaking as another climax builds.

I lose my mind completely, my fingers digging into her flushed, overheated skin as I feast on her like a beast. The wet sounds of my tongue lapping up her come, the way she pushes against me for more, the broken way she cries my name from behind that tape—it all drives me further, pushing me into a fucking frenzy.

Then, suddenly, her body snaps, shattering as her orgasm tears through her. I don't stop. I eat her twitching cunt and asshole, moving between them like I can't decide which one I want more of, both throbbing and glistening with the filthy mess I've drawn out of her.

Finally, I pull back, licking my lips, my breathing unsteady as I stare down. Her holes are red raw, swollen, pulsating with aftershocks. My eyes trail up to her face, her expression hazy and dazed, utterly destroyed—and I can't help but smirk.

"You're being so obedient for me, little sister. Something tells me you're enjoying every sinful second of this." I growl.

I reach between her legs, picking up the butt plug that's now dowsed in her dripping come. I glide it over her pussy, getting it nice and wet before pressing it against her asshole. She sucks in a sharp breath as I twist and push, easing it in, until finally, she swallows the entire thing, her pink ring tucked around it, holding it in place.

After taking in the fluffy bunny tail still attached, I move the string of her panties back in place, between her red cheeks. I shove on her outer thigh with my palm, making her fall and she rolls onto her back.

CHAPTER TWELVE

Ebony

Breathing heavily, my blue eyes find his green ones as he crawls up my sweaty body, between my spread legs.

Fuck, what the hell did he just do to me? This isn't the Rook I know, or is it? It's not like we explored much together. But it's like he's punishing me, yet he doesn't know that whatever he's doing, it's only giving me everything I want and more.

His arm sneaks around the middle of my back, arching me toward him, and he lowers his face toward my tits.

"I've always loved these big tits," he snarls.

His teeth graze over the thin fabric that covers my nipple as he holds eye contact. He gently bites down on it and lifts it, peeling it away from my skin, completely exposing me.

As soon as my hardened tip is free, he flattens his warm, wet tongue against it, stroking it with a flick before taking it into his mouth. My eyes flutter shut as he starts to devour it, his hand now sneaking into the waistband of my panties and grazing over my sensitive clit.

He continues to sink lower until he's slipping his fingers inside my pussy, and I gasp, feeling how strange it is with my ass full of the butt plug. He presses against it as if he wanted to feel it for himself, then he eases them out of me again.

His hand moves up, pinching the corner of the tape, and ripping it off my tingling lips with a quick pull. The sudden string shocks my senses, and I almost scream.

"Motherfucker!" I hiss, shooting him a sharp, fiery glare.

But when his smirk spreads, taunting and cruel, I lift my hand, ready to strike—like I always do—but before I can, his grip snatches my wrist, slamming it down beside me with brutal force.

"That smart mouth is gonna get it fucked." His voice is a growl, but his eyes are still filled with dark amusement. "It was only a little upper lip wax... Not like you didn't need—"

I don't let him finish. My other hand swipes, aiming for the blow, but again, he's faster. He catches my second wrist, pinning both of them above my head with one giant hand, holding me there like I'm nothing—helpless, his prisoner.

I fight against him, writhing, but he ignores it, his eyes locked on something beside us and my gaze follows his, drawn to the glint of a black, shiny half-bunny mask. I pause, and my pulse quickens as he brings it toward my face, securing it behind my head.

When it's in place, he takes me in, his eyes devouring me like a predator sizing up his prey. The mask hides half my face, leaving only my lips exposed, and as he stares, loving the sight of me, I start to feel my body melt again.

"Now what?" His voice drops, a taunt in the air. "You're just my helpless little fucking bunny this Christmas."

Before I can even open my mouth to throw some sass back, his lips crash against mine, hard and demanding. It's not a kiss—it's an assault. His tongue shoves past my lips, plunging down my throat with force, until I'm gasping for air, surrendering to him, kissing him back with equal hunger.

It doesn't take long before it becomes savage again—like it always does. His free hand rips my bra upward, exposing both of my breasts, my nipples brushing his tattooed skin. Then, his fingers working hurriedly between us, unbuckling his belt and in an instant, his big cock is freed, thick and heavy.

With a rough push, he moves my panties aside, the cold air biting at my exposed, wet pussy. His pierced tip brushes against my entrance briefly before he thrusts into me, unapologetic, punishing, taking me with one heartless plunge.

I can't hold back the cry that leaves my throat, but his mouth continues to attack mine, muffling the sound. The pressure inside me—his massive cock and the butt plug—feels like too much, an overload that pushes me to the corners of madness. My body shudders, unable to process the devastating sensation, but he doesn't give a shit. He groans, low and animalistic, before pulling back and slamming into me with a violent force, burying himself deep, carelessly driving in and out, hate fucking me.

Each savage stroke pushes me further into a dizzying spiral, my big tits bouncing wildly against his chest. The chains above us rattle with every hard fuck, swinging in time with his punishing rhythm, the bells around my throat annoyingly jingling in the same sync.

"Fuck," he growls with pleasure, his breath hot against my lips. "Between your tight cunt and that plug, you're squeezing the life out of my cock, Eb."

My legs instinctively lock around his waist, pulling him closer, my body begging for more, despite how full I feel. I yield to him, surrendering, each nerve alive with the desperate need for the sinful pleasure only he can provide.

Without a word, he releases my wrists, his hand slipping into the back of my hair, grabbing a fistful and yanking my head back causing me to hiss. His other hand wraps around the front of my throat, dulling the sound of the bells, attempting to silence everything but the wetness of him inside me.

He holds me still, dominating me, as his light green eyes burn into mine, watching every second.

"Open your fucking mouth," he bites out forcefully, his teeth grazing my lips. "Let me spit in that slut throat of yours."

I obey without hesitation, caught in a haze of euphoria that clouds my mind, making me forget everything but him and my lip's part, letting him have his way with me.

"Wider. Tongue out."

I do as he says, my breath shallow, the pleasure building in my body with every devastating thrust. Catching me off guard, he spits directly into my throat, and the sharpness of it almost makes me gag, but his hold tightens instantly, cutting off my air supply, suffocating me into submission.

The humiliation is shameful, the degradation and pain blending with the pleasure, spiraling together. My orgasm builds rapidly, the compression in my head blurring every thought and my nails rake down his tattooed back, drawing blood, begging for even a shred of empathy.

"Only when you come for me, little sister, will I let you breathe the same air as me again," he whispers darkly, his voice a hiss. "This is your big brother hate fucking the life out of you, just as your deserve."

My face turns to a deep purple, eyes nearly bulging from my head as he holds me at the edge—teetering between life and death. He doesn't stop, no matter how much I tear his skin apart, he doesn't show sympathy, letting me spiral dangerously close to the point of no return. But he keeps his word, waiting, until finally, I shatter.

The moment my body jerks violently, caught in the intense, overpowering waves of an orgasm, he releases his hold on my throat, and the sudden rush of air into my lungs intensifies the pleasure. I gasp, choking before the sound of a strangled, untamed scream escapes my throat, the sensation consuming me.

Then I feel it—something I now find hard to hold onto—the hot, pulsing release. The pressure in my core builds to an unbearable peak causing my pussy to squirt all over him in hot, messy sprays. It soaks his lower body, but it only drives him wilder, more feral.

Without hesitation, he shifts, bracing himself up on one arm, hovering over me, as his free hand finds my clit, rubbing it hard and fast. The stimulation sends my come flying, drenching both of us even more, and I arch violently, my back bending in oversensitivity until I feel him bury as deep as he can, his cock swelling and jerking inside me.

He collapses on top of me, his heavy weight knocking the air from my small body. His chest presses against mine, hot and suffocating, as he empties himself. The feeling of his cum filling me up makes my thighs tremble around him and we lie there, still, both of us trying to process the chaos we've just shared.

His breaths come heavy against my hair, but I can't help running my hands up his toned back, fingers tracing the inked skin, unable to stop myself from touching him, claiming whatever part of him I can.

My heart pounds, a frenzied rhythm, as my thoughts swirl—about him, about us, about what comes after this. What does he want from this? Is it just another filthy night to add to the naughty list, and then we part ways, as if nothing happened until the next time? Or are we done after this? The idea that I could be pulled into something I don't want, a deeper connection that will never be mine to keep, fills me with an aching sadness.

And the thought of Rook—of him being with someone else who could never fill the void he carries in his heart for me—pulls at me in ways I can't explain.

Suddenly, he moves, pushing himself off me, giving me a much-needed air. He sits back on his knees, his eyes locking with mine, his expression unreadable, as his chin tilts upward, full of that darkness I know all too well. There's no softness in his gaze, no hint of the connection we just shared, only coldness. It's clear he hates me right now.

He tucks his cock away in his boxers, zipping up his jeans but leaving the belt undone, as if the moment we shared means nothing. When he's finished, he reaches out, adjusting my lingerie back into place, but he doesn't look at me. Then he moves away, making his way to the doors and stepping out of the van.

My eyes follow him as he stands outside in the snow, his back to me, lighting a cigarette and the ember glows briefly, casting a faint light on his face. I even forgot the doors have been wide open this entire time. The heat between us seems to melt away the blizzard outside.

I sit up carefully, the bells around my neck chiming softly, betraying my movement. Rook side-eyes me as I reach for his leather jacket and wrap it around my near-naked body, then crawl toward him. Then, his focus fixes on some point ahead, taking another deep drag of his cigarette.

When I'm at the edge of the van, I gently jump down into the snow, my boots crunching against the frozen ground. I almost slip but catch myself, steadying my steps until I stop behind him.

I slip my arms around the front of his toned body, loving his warmth, even though he's shirtless and standing in the biting cold. Snowflakes fall and melt against his tattooed skin, the way I do when I touch him—lingering, then lost.

He inhales sharply as I press a kiss to his back, then growls low, a warning. "I'm not here for all that or to fall deeper in love with you, Bunny. That's not what tonight is about. I'm here to fuck you out of my system and let us both move on with our lives."

His words hit harshly, stabbing into my heart and I retreat slightly, unease creeping in. "Move on?" I murmur, loosening my hold on him, insecurity twisting through me.

He turns to face me, his eyes cold and distant, and I tilt my head back, meeting his gaze, snowflakes kissing my lips.

"Yeah," he says, his voice hard and biting. "You can go live your happily ever after, and I'll settle down with some poor chick who'll never even come close to matching my sister. That's how it was always gonna be, right?"

His words sting, sharper than they ever have. I don't let him see it though, I lower my eyes quickly, hiding the hurt before he can catch it.

"Some chick?" I repeat quietly, the annoyance creeping in like an old friend.

But it's always been this way. Rook's possessiveness has always been way too much, suffocating at times, loud, but I've been just as jealous—only I kept it hidden. The only difference is, he's always had the freedom to do whatever the fuck he wanted with other women. Me? I had men picked for me, like I was some damn object.

"Am I not allowed to be with other women when you've been fucking Blaise?" His accusation is like a dagger, and my brows lift in surprise by the spite in his words.

"Tell me, big brother," I say, my voice calm but laced with a challenge, "how much have you been watching me?" I raise an eyebrow, crossing my arms tightly over my chest. "Because if you were stalking me hard enough, you'd know I haven't fucked a single man since that Christmas two years ago. You're the only one I've ever been with."

He doesn't react at first. Instead, he takes another long suck of his cigarette, his dark eyes locked on mine as if searching for any sign of a lie, but I don't budge because it's the truth. I wait for an answer, but he just shrugs, the gesture careless.

"When it came to you and guys… I couldn't do it." He exhales, the smoke curling from his lips like his words. "When you started getting serious with Blaise, I stopped watching you altogether."

"Serious?" I echo, my brows furrowing, disbelief and frustration mixing. "Do you really think any of these guys are what I want? Nothing will ever be fucking serious."

A heavy silence settles between us and my heart throbs, an ache I can't ignore, but I hold his gaze, steadying myself. "As you said, none of these poor men will ever match to my big brother."

He stares into my eyes, his jaw clenched tight, like he's holding back wrath. "And it took you all this fucking time to finally admit that? When I was bleeding for you, you shot me down and made me feel like it was all in my head."

My throat tightens and I can feel my eyes welling up, the memory of that night crashing over me again—how heartbroken he was, how I shattered him when I didn't want to.

"I don't want to hear it anymore, Ebony," he mutters, shaking his head as if the thought disgusts him. "You fuck with my head. Drove me insane. You throw me these mixed signals time and time again. You tell me everything I want to hear when we're alone, but when shit gets real, you fucking bail on me. You've never fought for this. You've never fought for us. And I can't do it alone."

He flicks his cigarette away before his cold fingers lock around my jaw, forcing my face up and his smoky lips brush over mine as he leans in.

"This Christmas is the end of us, little sister." His tone is heavy with finality. "It's how it all started, and it's how it'll finish. So, soak it the fuck up, because this will never happen between us again."

I search his eyes, a single tear slipping from mine, and in that moment, his gaze drops to my lips. He suddenly releases me, his touch gone as quickly as it came and he moves past me without a second glance, leaving me on the edge of breaking down.

But before I can even crumble, his arm snakes around my waist, yanking me back against him. In one swift, effortless motion, he lifts me into the van, lowering us onto the fur covered floor. He leans back against the van's metal shell, tucking me sideways between his legs, and the weight of the butt plug inside me makes me feel uncomfortable.

He slips the leather jacket from my shoulders again, uncovering me to the biting chill. "Remember that Christmas when you broke your big toe?" His voice is softer now, his fingers brushing my hair aside, exposing the side of my neck.

I scoff, looking away. "You mean when you broke my big toe."

"No, bunny. You broke it when you kicked me."

"Yeah, because you tore the head off my new limited-edition Barbie and fed it to the dog!" I snap, my eyes narrowing as I glare up at him.

A devilish smirk spreads across his lips, handsomely beautiful. "Damn right I fucking did." His gaze flickers between my lips and my eyes, his tone dripping. "You sat there staring at that plastic piece of shit for hours, calling it the most beautiful thing in the world."

His expression darkens as he leans in, his voice almost a growl. "Like fuck I'd let my little sister think anything compares to her. So, yeah. I ripped her head off, fed it to the mutt, and laughed while doing it." His fingers comb through the back of my hair, achingly gentle. "After that, it was just you again—the only thing that's ever been perfect. And I'll destroy anything that makes you forget it. Every. Fucking. Time."

I stare into his eyes, my heart pounding, my mind racing. "Why the fuck are you telling me this, Rook?" My voice trembles, not with fear but with frustration. "You just made your feelings perfectly clear that this ends tonight."

"I just want you to know," he murmurs, "you were my sister before you were anything else. And I'll always be the person you fucking need. You don't always have to be flawless, Bunny. You don't have to always be perfect—to be perfect to me."

His words strike a chord, hitting somewhere deep. He knows I always strive for perfection—it's woven into my veins, drilled into my mind for as long as I can remember. I have to choose perfection, look perfection, speak perfection. But with Rook, perfection has never mattered. He's seen me at my worst, unashamedly. All my sharp edges and broken pieces. He's seen how feisty I can be, how bare, how silly, how messy, and completely disorganized.

Around him, I've never had to keep up that façade. I've never had to hide. He's the one person who's seen the chaos inside me and held it like it was something precious, something worthy of love. Worthy of his love.

I lift my hand to his face, aiming for the small black piece of tape under his left eye that's been bothering me all night.

"What the fuck is this?" I mutter.

Before he can react, I rip it off his face, and he hisses sharply, causing me to smirk. But my amusement fades the second I see what's underneath. My face falls, and my hand flies to cover my open mouth.

"Rook… is that—?"

His piercing green eyes snap to mine, gauging my reaction. My fingers tremble as I reach for his face again, my thumb brushing over the small black bunny mask tattoo inked beneath his eye.

"Please tell me that's fake," I gasp, my voice shaky as I meet his gaze.

His throat bobs as he swallows hard, then he gives me a small, almost faint shake of his head.

"I got it just after I left. I wanted to carry a part of you with me, despite the pain."

My thoughts whirl, emotions clashing. He has something that represents me permanently marked on his face? That's insane. I can't even begin to process it. It's so strangely romantic of him.

"Don't worry, I regretted it almost immediately," he says, his lips twitching into a wicked smirk, teasing me.

I force a smile in return, but it feels brittle, like it might shatter if he looks too closely. As I become lost in thought, I start to think it's best we get this night over with before he shreds my heart to pieces completely. He wants me for one more measly Christmas night?

Fine. Let's give the plague a night he'll never forget.

CHAPTER THIRTEEN

ROOK

Suddenly, Ebony moves, lifting herself until she's straddling my lap frontally. Her thighs press against mine, the heat of her pussy against me unmistakable, even through the fabric. My brows pinch as she settles, her blue eyes locked on me from behind her bunny mask.

Without a word, her fingers reach to the side, plucking up a candy cane that I had hidden and while holding my gaze, she peels away the wrapper, her lips curving into a sinister grin.

"Remember when we used to fight over the last one of these?" she purrs, pressing her big tits against my chest, her soft curves testing my restraint.

I raise an expressionless eyebrow, trying to play it down. "When didn't we fight over everything?"

Her smirk widens, teasing before her tongue darts out, slowly sliding along the length of the candy cane. She flicks over the tip before taking it into her mouth, the motion shameless and seductive as she sinks it deep to the back of her throat. I feel all my blood surge to my dick in an instant as my grip tightens on her thick thighs.

When she pulls it out with a soft, wet pop, she bites her bottom lip, her gaze shimmering with mischief.

"Maybe we can share this Christmas," she whispers, her voice like silk, her lashes fluttering. "Or maybe..." Her eyes flicker downward as she continues, hips bucking against me, grinding her cunt over my length. "I can do the same to your cock, big brother? I've always wondered what you'd taste like in my mouth."

A low growl rumbles from my chest before I grab a handful of her hair, yanking her head to the side. Her sinister grin only grows, gleaming with satisfaction as I reach down, yanking my zipper open with my free hand. My palm dips into my boxers, wrapping around my throbbing dick, pulling it free. Her eyes drop instantly, drinking in the sight, lingering on the glint of my piercing as I stroke myself downward.

Without hesitation, I guide her head, and she doesn't resist—in fact, she leans in, eager, her lips parting as she accepts me in. As soon as she wraps around the tip, I can't stop the sharp inhale I take from the sensation. Far too many times have I thought about her giving me head or me skull fucking her, and here she is, willingly just doing it.

Her lips slide downward, taking me with a soft moan, enjoying every inch as I hit the back of her throat before coming back up. She doesn't rush, no, just tasting me and my toes curl in my boots, the sight and feel of her driving me to the verge of no return.

"That's it. Suck it like you love the taste of your big brother's dick down your throat." I grit, taking a deep breath.

Both my hands find her hair, clutching tightly as I fight to keep control, the pleasure threatening to take over. Her tongue flicks over the tip as she releases, her hand guiding the candy cane to the side of my shaft.

Then she lowers her mouth again, sucking me and the candy in together, her eyes flicking upward to meet mine. Those crystal blue eyes—dark with intent—watch me come apart. She knows exactly what she's fucking doing. She's playing me at my own game.

The overwhelming sensation is too much, and I find myself regretting my words. The way her mouth repeatedly swallows my cock like it's meant to be there, leaves me panting.

"Don't do that," I hiss through teeth clenched, back tracking, as a sharp shudder ripples through me.

She pulls back just enough to grin, her lips grazing the tip. "Do what?"

My jaw tightens, my grip on her hair firm as I spit out the words.

"Suck my dick like you know how to. Like you were fucking made for it. I'm gonna shoot my load up your face in 0.2 seconds and give a whole new meaning to snow blow."

She maintains her smile as she licks her tongue over my piercing, her breath hot against it. "You like it, don't you? When you feel the back of your sister's throat?"

With that, she sucks me back into her mouth, this time harder, rougher, and quicker, pushing me to my limits. The peppermint burns against my cock as she takes me further, her head bobbing wildly. My hold on her hair tightens, ripping strands from her scalp and my breathing turns heavy as I fight the need to take over completely.

When her sighs vibrate against me, I can't hold back any longer. I move, getting on my knees in front of her, but her mouth doesn't leave me for a second, eager and needy, she follows. She pulls the candy cane out just as I grab the back of her head with both hands, forcing myself deeper.

She gags instantly, her throat squeezing around me as the bells on her neck jingle with every thrust. I snarl low, slamming into her harder and faster, my control completely snapped. Her eyes water, but she takes it. Her nails dig into my thighs, clinging to me as if she needs this as much as I do.

Her lips are tight around the thick girth, and the wet, filthy sounds she makes drives me fucking insane. I gaze down at her, watching how her plump lips move over every vein and curve, leaving a sloppy wetness in her wake. My head falls back briefly, my eyes rolling, the sight of her wrecked face burned into my mind.

Her mouth grows wetter, saliva spilling and dripping onto the fur beneath us, struggling to take my violent plunges, but I don't give a shit. With my hands holding her in place on the back of her head, I smash into her cruelly, making her take every inch to the base until finally, I cum.

My cock jerks violently, and I bury myself in her throat, forcing her to swallow every last drop. Her tonsils tighten around my piercing as I ride the waves of release, my entire body tingling from head to toe.

When I pull out, she gasps desperately for air, and I grab her face, tilting her head back so our eyes lock. Tears stream down her flushed cheeks, her lips swollen and slick with my cum, and the sight of her shocked and ruined makes my cock twitch all over again.

"You fucking asked for that," I growl, watching her smile despite the tears streaking her face.

She pushes herself up onto her knees, wrapping her arms around my neck and pulling me into a heated kiss. Her lips are soft and sticky, and when she backs away just enough to murmur, her words are pure sin.

"You taste exactly like I thought you would, Rook. Fucking satanic."

I lift a brow, amusement flickering in my eyes. I've never seen this side of Ebony before—the one who takes control. After two long years, there's something different about her. She's still my Ebony, but now she's growing into a woman with a backbone. It kills me to think that strength evaporates the moment her dad comes into the picture.

She releases me and leans down, carefully picking up my plague mask from the floor. When she hands it to me, I take it without a word, staring down at it.

A symbol of who I've been outside this hell. *The Plague.* Ruthless. Unforgiving. Deadly. A side of me she's never seen. A side that has been created throughout all this. It's what they've called me for two years now—though she clearly doesn't know that.

"I want you to chase me in it again," she says softly, her voice laced with something daring and my eyes snap to hers.

152

"I liked it when you chased me... and took what you wanted. It made me feel alive."

The darkness stirring in her blue gaze, pulls me in. Watching. Waiting. Challenging me.

I slip the mask on, the familiar burden settling over me. Her lips curl into a sly smile before she backs away, holding eye contact as she steps out of the van. The snow swirls around her nearly naked figure, the delicate lingerie clinging to her body. Then, like a ghost on Christmas night, she's gone.

I take a deep inhale, grabbing my cane, the lights wrapped around it still flickering wildly. Then, I pursue her, hopping out the van and listening for the bells around her throat. I hear them in the distance to my right and I start to walk that way, the heavy snowfall making it hard to see

I trudge through, my boots squishing as they sink into the softened ground, each step bringing me closer. The forest looms ahead, dark and quiet, except for the faint jingle of her bells. They taunt me like Santa's sleigh, urging me forward, and I smirk beneath my mask.

As I enter the woods, my eyes scanning the ground. Her little footprints dot the snow like breadcrumbs, guiding me to where she's hiding, and the chime of her bells starts to grow louder. My breath fogs the mask as I move faster, my pulse quickening with the thrill of the hunt.

Suddenly, the sound stops, and so do I. My senses sharpen, eyes darting around the silent trees and the forest holds its breath, the tension crackling. My heart pounds as I listen, still as stone—until I spot her.

She darts from behind a tree, a flash of movement, trying to reach another hiding spot. Her giggle cuts through the silence, light and playful. I raise a brow at her audacity, amused by her little game, how carefree she is.

I follow, quickening my steps, watching her every move. She dashes from tree to tree, her bells clinking with each step, her ass swaying, the bunny tail still intact and her tits bounce up and down. She knows exactly what she's doing, playing with me, enjoying the chase as much as I do.

I close in, and just when she thinks she's made it to another tree, I make my presence known. My cane sweeps through the air, hooking her legs. She stumbles with a startled yelp, but before she can hit the ground, I grab her hair and yank her against me.

She screams, her back colliding with my front, warm and soft against the cold. My hand shoots to her throat, gripping the delicate skin, holding her firmly in place. She squirms, her breath hitching as I lean down, my mouth grazing her ear.

"Oh, look," I growl. "I caught myself a pretty little bunny this Christmas."

I shove her forward again until she staggers, collapsing onto her hands and knees in the snow. I close the distance, the tip of my glowing cane pressing firmly against the fur covered plug nestled inside her asshole. Her body shudders, her fingers curling into the freezing slush as if preparing herself.

My cock swells again at the sight of her—bent over, obedient, fucking slut. Ready to be ruined by me. I raise the cane high, then bring it down hard against her asscheek. The crack echoes in the cold night, and she screams, her body jerking forward from the force. Before she can crumble completely, I lunge, my fist grabbing the back of her panties and yanking her roughly back onto all fours.

"You want to know what it's really like to be fucked by your big brother, little bunny?" My voice drips with menace, every word a threat and promise. "Then get ready to meet the plague you created and begged for."

She's panting, the sting of the strike still etched across her skin, burning a bright red and I can see the mix of pain and need radiating from her. I crouch behind her, shifting the cane in my hand, and without hesitation, I press the thick, glowing tip to her wet cunt. Slowly, I drag it upward, parting her lips and her body fights to take the unrelenting pressure.

A broken whimper escapes her as she reaches back in desperation and I release her panties, swatting her hand away with a sharp snarl.

"Don't."

The second she lowers her hand, I grab the thin lace of her panties again, ripping them with a vicious tug that sends her jolting forward before I pull her back into place again, wrapping them around my fist so she can't escape what I'm about to do to her. Her spine arches beautifully, every line of her body a picture of surrender. I press the cane forward again, this time with more force, the glowing light flickering against her pink, swollen lips as her cunt gives way to take the cane inside.

Her moans cuts through the icy air as I drive it deeper, the lights disappearing inside her one by one, inch by agonizing inch, until I pause, letting her feel the full weight of it embedded inside her. My growl reverberates, low and savage, as I savor the moment.

Then, I begin to work the cane in and out of her, steady at first, the little bulbs flashing erratically each time they disappear inside her wet, slutty pussy. The soaked, obscene sound of her taking it fills the air, mingling with her small whimpers and my heavy breathing.

My fingers tighten on her shredded panties, using them as reins to keep her bound and under control, pulling sharply to arch her back as I start to ram deeper, forcing her to take more inside her with every savage thrust.

My movements grow feral, the tempo ruthless and remorseless. Each plunge draws a cry from her lips, her trembling legs threatening to give out under the sheer force of it.

"Such a greedy little pussy," I snarl.

Finally, she breaks. A strangled scream erupts from her as her orgasm crashes over her, her body convulsing under the weight of her release. The sight is hypnotic—her surrender, real and unfiltered, as she quakes in my hold.

It's going to be so fucking hard to let her go. She's made for me and every sick, disgusting fantasy I have.

I finally rip the cane out of her pulsing, dripping pussy before letting her go and she falls forward on release, crashing into the melting snow. I stand carefully before moving around her body, noticing how unbothered she is against the freezing cold, just like I am. The heat and adrenaline between us is keeping us well and truly alive.

I toss my cane onto the floor, the sharp crack of it landing making her flinch. I stop just inches from her, my breath shallow. My eyes flick up to the branch above me, where a long, thick icicle dangles, a cruel weapon of winter.

I reach for it, tearing it free with a sharp, crackling twist, the cold biting into my hand. She lifts her head, her gaze finding me as I lower myself, lying back on the cold floor. The wetness from the icy ground soaks into my back, but it's irrelevant—nothing matters but her.

I crook a finger at her, both our eyes locked from behind our masks.

"Now crawl to me, little sister. Ride my mask while I fuck your ass with this icicle." I command, my voice rough, hungry, breathless.

Her body trembles, but she doesn't disobey. She rises up onto her hands and knees, her movements almost hesitant, before she starts to crawl toward me. I watch her hips and dangling tits sway with each step. When she leans over me, her eyes search my body, pausing on the sharp beak of my mask.

"That's not going to fit..." she says, her voice breaking, but I snarl in response. I drop the icicle to the side, grip her waist tightly and turn her effortlessly. I lift her, positioning her until she's backward, her body arched above mine, her thighs pressed to my chest.

I tilt my head, the jagged edge of the beak of my mask pressing against her leaking, battered pussy. She gasps, her nails digging into my legs, but I don't let her escape. I grasp her waist and force her down onto the mask, making her cunt take it. She lets out a dragging cry, struggling to take it.

"No. No. Don't you dare cry," I warn, my voice harsh, muffled behind the leather. "No tears. The only sound I want from that big mouth of yours is a symphony of moans—rough, desperate, fucking mine. You're going to take this mask. Every curve of that beak. I want your come dripping, spilling through the eyeholes, until it's all I taste."

"But..." she gasps, breath shaky, "I already feel so full... with this plug inside me..."

Without warning, I grip the butt plug, twisting it cruelly in my hand before yanking it free. Her legs tense around me, her body shuddering violently as the emptiness inside her throbs and I watch, mesmerized, as her asshole pulses, gaping open from the absence of the large object.

Her pussy smears come down the length of the beak, and my cock twitches in response. I reach beside me for the icicle, my fingers brushing against the cold edge. My other hand grabs her hip before I force her down gently, making her cunt take more of the mask.

I observe, captivated, as she sinks lower, the beak spreading her pussy lips impossibly wide around the leather, each movement making her pant. She takes it at her own pace, but the pace is mine to command.

"Oh, my god… It's so big… and sharp," she gasps, her breath hitching as she pushes herself beyond her limits.

"Such a good little whore for your big brother," I rasp, watching her body fall apart above me. "Your pussy looks so fucking beautiful, stretched and eager around my mask."

I can smell her arousal, thick and heady, as it drips down onto me, leaking through the sockets. When she's taken nearly all of it, she starts to rise, lifting her hips, before sliding back down, riding the mask with desperate, frantic thrusts. I growl, the sight so intoxicating, I can't look away.

"That's it, fuck it. Destroy your little cunt for me."

With the thick icicle in my hand, its coldness seeping into my palm, I press my free hand against her back, shoving her further onto the mask. Then, I ease the long icy shaft into her ass, the cold biting against her warmth, making her body tremble violently. She screws her pussy, the freezing cold intrusion spreading her further as I start to fuck her with it at the same time.

Her moans grow louder, more hysterical, the sound of her pleasure nearly drowning out everything else. The icicle melts rapidly inside her, the liquid warmth pouring down, splashing onto my mask and soaking my skin beneath her as I fuck her relentlessly.

The entire position, the filthy intimacy of what we're doing, the sounds of her sloppy pussy, almost makes me cum in my jeans. I feel myself snapping again, my sanity slipping. She gets carried away for some time, stretching her cunt to its absolute limit, ruining herself right in front of me, slamming herself down onto my face, her weight crushing the air from my lungs.

When her body finally slows down, I reach over, grabbing a handful of snow. My other hand presses firmly against her back again, forcing her to bend lower, holding her in place. Without hesitation, I begin shoving the snow into her ass, each thrust sinking deeper, each motion adding another finger.

One,

Two,

Three.

Only when her ass is stuffed to the brim with snow, I start finger fucking her at the same time, my hand relentless, water squirting everywhere. The sensations overwhelm her; the cold, the pressure, and my fingers plunging, it's too much.

"Fuckkkkk..." she screams.

She collapses forward as she climaxes unexpectedly, but my mask remains lodged halfway inside her pussy, her come flooding down it as I continue to ruin her ass, the snow melting against her heat, the violent pleasure shattering her completely.

But I don't stop. I don't care. I push her further. I love to see her body overwhelmed and I'm the one doing it.

I tear my mask from her and my face, tossing it aside, and look down at her limp body between my legs. Grabbing another handful of snow, I haul her up onto her knees again. Her protests are nothing but broken gasps as I start to shove the snow inside her cunt as well, her body jerking with every cold plunge.

"Let's numb this battered pussy with snow, then you can take more of me."

The chill soothes and tortures her all at once, her trembling unstoppable in my hands.

When I'm finished, I press my fingers and thumb against her entrance. She hisses, her hand flying back to grab my wrist, her instinct to stop me weak. I don't hesitate, twisting and pressing, forcing her pussy to open as I attempt to get my hand inside. Her body resists, shaking violently.

"Relax and be a good girl, you can take it, bunny. It's just a little sting and my hand will be inside you." I breathe.

I don't relent. I ease in further until my knuckles sink just past her entrance, her pussy wide around them.

"Rook!" she shrieks in protest.

I pause, watching her pink, glistening cunt quiver, stretched impossibly tight around me, too tight. Her breathing comes in shaky gasps, and she lets out a strangled hiss as I begin to rotate my hand gently, the smooth glide of her tight, pink skin around my knuckles, perfect.

"That's the hottest shit I've ever fucking seen," I growl, my voice thick with satisfaction. "You were made for this, little sister."

Then, with a brutal motion, I tear my fist free from her pussy, knowing better than to shove my entire hand inside. She falls forward as soon as I let her go, gasping at the sudden emptiness, her body twitching at my feet.

"I think you've got some kind of deranged, sadistic stretch kink, Plague," she pants out, barely able to breathe."

"And I think you fucking love it." I respond calmly, running my hands over her cold ass, squeezing and splitting her wide so I can see how ruined and swollen she is.

I grip the front of her thighs, pulling her onto her knees again.

"God, come the fuck here. Smother your wrecked cunt all over my tongue and lips." I order with a growl; I'm far from finished.

She splits her legs wider, lowering herself and my tongue snakes out, lazily devouring her, slurping up all her come and the water inside her. She rocks back and forth, gliding her pussy all over my face, moaning softly, letting me soothe her.

When we're done here, I start to move. Snow falls in thick flakes around us as I rise, lifting her limp body into my arms. She sags over my shoulder, utterly exhausted. I lean down, gathering my cane and mask, then reach up and snap another icicle from a branch above.

Without a word, I carry her back to the van, the snow closing in behind us.

161

Ebony

Now we're back in the van and Rook has me chained to the ceiling again. I've been sitting on his knees behind me for what feels like hours, his hard cock sinking deep into my come-filled asshole as I ride him repeatedly.

His hands roam over my body, teasing my sensitive tits and soaked pussy with an icicle, while his tongue drags hot, wet lines along my neck, his teeth sinking into me now and then.

I moan, my head falling back against his shoulder, my eyes rolling in lust. His cold fingers dip between my thighs, finding my swollen clit, circling it lazily as the ice trails over my hardened nipple, making me shiver.

"So, fucking beautiful," he rasps in my ear, sending a wave of euphoria crashing over me. "I love you so much."

Suddenly, he reaches up and releases the chain. I lurch forward, but he catches me this time, guiding me down until my head is pressed low and my ass is high in the air. With a firm grip on my waist, he takes full control, driving his big cock into my ass over and over, her hands branding my hips with every forceful thrust.

He holds onto the moment, each movement unhurried. I open my tired eyes, gazing out of the open doors, seeing the sunset starting to rise over the snowy lake horizon. I side-eye as he leans over me, his hands braced either side of my head before he starts smashing his dick into my ass at a steepest position. I cry out, my eyes squeezing shut, but I let him have his way with me.

He finally comes for the last time, pushing deep, emptying himself, then he drags his dick out of me. I collapse as he falls beside me, pulling me into him.

I back myself up against his sweaty body and he lifts a thick fur blanket over us finally. With him up on his elbow, he stares down at me, stroking my hair away from my eyes. I gaze back, our silence speaking louder than words ever could, but I need to get shit off my chest.

"I'm sorry," I whisper, my voice broken. "I never got to say it to you. But all that I said that night, it wasn't how I really felt."

He doesn't move now, and I can't tell what he's thinking, can't dissect what's brewing behind that cold, unflinching façade of his. Frustration bubbles up, twisting with my pain and I shake my head once, the tears I've been holding back spilling over, but I don't care if he sees my weaknesses.

"I do love you, Rook," I finally admit. "I never stopped loving you. But I just couldn't—couldn't be with you."

He doesn't react right away and the quiet stretches between us, taut and suffocating. Then, his head tilts slightly.

"So why the fuck didn't you just say that?" His voice cuts through, but there's an accusing edge to it. "Why the hell did you say all that other crazy bullshit? We could of just…"

My lip wobbles as I exhale, bracing myself. "You know why," I say softly, barely able to meet his eyes. He stays still, waiting, and I realize he's not going to let me off the hook, so I continue.

"My dad," I finally murmur. "He gave me little choice. Either shut us down or…" My throat tightens, and I have to pause to swallow the sob that threatens to escape. "Or you die."

His head slants slightly, a motion so small but it makes me shiver.

"I would rather live my life away from you, through heartache, than never see your face again, Rook. It was an easy decision. Not because I didn't want to be with you, but because you being alive meant more to me than… than anything. Even more than our love. What I did—it wasn't fucking rejection. It wasn't anger. It wasn't hate. It was love. Every single thing I did was out of love."

"You overestimate your father and underestimate me, Bunny," he snaps, and his words land harsh, making my chest tighten. "Why don't you just let me kill that motherfucker for you? For me? And we can get on with what we both want—each other."

I shake my head, exhaustion sitting on me like a heavy chain. "I don't underestimate you, Rook; I know what you're capable of," I murmur, my gaze moving away. "But it's just not that simple. How would you feel if I said that about your mom? That I want to kill her?"

I look at him now above me, but he stays quiet, so I push forward, needing him to hear this. "We both know what it's like to lose a parent. Could we really live with losing another? Could our relationship survive when the only way we were able to stay together was by killing my only living parent?"

"He doesn't deserve you, Ebony," he finally seethes, and his fists clench, his entire body taut with rage. "He's making you fucking miserable. The only reason I haven't killed him yet is for your sake."

I drop my gaze because I know he's right. I know every word he says is the truth, and it eats at me because I don't have a solution. No matter how much I've thought about it—tortured myself over it—I've never found a way out.

"Well, I wanted to spend one last Christmas with you, Eb," he murmurs. "For old times' sake. Then I'd let you go. I can't keep seeing you like this. This… broken."

The words hit me like a punch to the stomach and I swallow hard, the ache in my chest intensifying as another tear threatens to spill.

"But it's not what I fucking want," he says, full of raw honesty and he lifts his hand to my face. I lean into it instinctively, closing my eyes to absorb his touch like it's a lifeline.

"But I'd rather you have a little bit of control in your life than none at all," he adds and before I can respond, his hand moves to wrap around my throat, and I open my eyes again, locking with his and everything else fades into nothing. He dips closer, his lips grazing mine, our breath mingling in a moment that feels like everything and nothing at once.

"Because I'm not going to let you keep being miserable," he murmurs. "That's how much I fucking love you. And if that means going back to just being your supportive big brother, then so be it. I was your brother before we became this and I just want to see you happy, Bunny."

My heart hurts, every part of me falling apart. He's not letting me go. He's offering me a way out, something to ease the hurt of what my life is going to become—but it's not freedom. No matter how this ends. I lose.

"I'm not going to be another reason you're suffocating anymore," he finishes, and a tear slips from the corner of my eye, burning its way down my cheek. "It's time to let each other go."

I hate every second of this because he's right—that's why I've always loved him so much. I suddenly lift myself and slam my lips against his, kissing him hard enough for him to know how I feel, how I really feel. He responds instantly, pressing his tongue into my mouth as his hand slides around the side of my neck, thumb dragging down the line of my jaw.

CHAPTER FOURTEEN

- NEW YEAR'S EVE -

ROOK

I sit on the edge of my bed, elbows propped on my knees, eyes locked on my laptop, though I'm not really seeing anything. My mind is somewhere else, drifting. Bunny steps into her room, her towel clinging to her wet skin, droplets of water trailing down her exposed back. She's getting ready for her dad's New Year's Eve party, and I can't help but notice how effortlessly beautiful she looks in that moment.

Yeah, I got invited too. But will I go? Fuck no. Since that night, I've been fighting tooth and nail to keep my distance. It's harder now than ever before. When she fell asleep in that van, all broken and vulnerable, I drove her home without a word, scooped her fragile little body up, and laid her gently on her bed in her apartment.

I lingered for a while, just watching her, feeling the weight of everything that had happened between us. Everything she said, everything we did, and all the things she admitted that, honestly, I wish she fucking didn't. For years, that's all I wanted. For her to finally say those words I'd been dying to hear. To hear her voice telling me that everything I felt—every twisted, obsessive part of it—wasn't just some sick fantasy in my head. That I wasn't imagining things, that it wasn't just a reflection of my own insanity.

But now? Now it's more complicated than I ever thought.

She loved me. She does love me. But she hid it—locked it away as deep as she could. She tried to protect us both in some fucked-up way, like it was some kind of shield against the unavoidable. But that's never what I wanted. I never asked for any of that. And now, it's not enough. It'll never be enough.

I can't keep holding out for her to come to her senses, for her "maybe" to turn into something solid, something real. I can't keep waiting for her to finally choose me. It's been eating me alive for too long. So, I did what I told myself I would. I let her go—well, at least, I told myself I did.

But the truth is I'm still right here, watching her every move, like some kind of desperate fucking ghost, unable to pull myself away. It's like a bad habit—something I can't quit, no matter how much I know it's killing me.

Ebony sits at the end of the bed, her eyes blank, staring into nothing. She's as miserable as always, but there's something about the way she sits, so fucking empty, that makes my chest tighten, makes me feel like I'm crumbling right along with her. I hate how much it affects me because I just want to give her everything to make her happy.

After a while, she picks up the hair dryer and I watch her—my eyes glued to her, unable to look away—until, just as I'm about to close the laptop and let myself slip back into my own darkness, she glances at the screen, clearly realizing the red light for her camera is on.

She never would've seen it before. She wouldn't have cared. But now, she does. She knows I'm watching her. I see it in the way her eyes harden, the slight pause before she turns off the dryer.

She sets it down, and for a moment, she sits there, her back turned, like she's deciding whether or not to confront me. Then, gently, she edges to the corner of the bed. Her eyes flick to me, dark and calculating, wondering if it's really me watching.

Then she does something that makes my heart skip a beat. She bites her lip, and I feel it—something's going to happen.

I don't know what comes over her, but she starts unfolding the towel, her movements slow, as if she's enjoying every second of this twisted little show she's putting on for me.

I inhale sharply, my eyes sweeping over her naked body. It's like a pull, magnetic and unstoppable. She knows it too—how the sight of her makes my blood run hot, how every inch of her is pure fucking sin. She leans back, placing one hand on the bed for support. She lifts her legs, flattening her feet on the bed, then splays them wide, as if offering herself.

I grind my teeth, my cock straining against my jeans, painfully solid. My body reacts before my mind can catch up, and I reach for it, the pressure almost unbearable.

"Shit," I mutter, my hand squeezing my dick as if telling it to calm the fuck down.

She stares into the lens, dragging her thumb over her tongue, down her bottom lip, and continuing until she's teasing her nipple with it. Her head tilts back, black hair cascading over her shoulders as she cups her pussy, pressing her fingers through her lips. Her hips buck against them, and it's probably one of the sexiest things I've ever seen.

I can hear her moans, even though the microphone's off as she rubs her fingers up and down her slit, pleasuring her needy little pussy just for me. Her head lifts, eyes glazed, her bottom lip between her teeth. Then, she fans her fingers out, splitting her pussylips open and wide, exposing herself fully. My gaze immediately drops to her clit, the glistening hole of her cunt, and I growl, my body tensing, desperate to be fucking her hard again.

My leg taps impatiently as she slides her fingers into herself, lazy and sensual, each stroke pushing her closer to the edge. She withdraws, bringing her soaked fingers to her lips, sucking them into her mouth, tasting herself before pulling them out and flipping me off with the middle one, a wicked smile spreading over her lips.

"Little fucking tease," I seethe.

She keeps going, fingering her pussy, but the more she does it, the harder it gets for me. I know I need to pull away, to stop this before I lose it completely. I close my eyes, willing myself to just let her go. Until, finally, I grab my laptop and slam the screen shut, the sound echoing through my room with finality. I stand with a frustrated snarl, turning quickly, anger burning through me, and storm out of my bedroom.

Ebony

When the red light suddenly blinks off on my laptop, I freeze, my face falling. A wave of humiliation washes over me as I close my legs and lower them before sitting up, my eyes fluttering shut.

"Fuck," I whisper, realizing this is it.

Rook has officially given up and who could blame him? I was stupid for playing that game, immature even, but I haven't been able to get him out of my mind since that night.

I've text him. I've tried to call, but he's just not answering me. He said he would still be my big brother, but maybe I'm just being pushy because deep down, I know, this isn't what I want. I don't want him to just be my big brother. I want him. All of him. All of us.

My eyes sting with unshed tears, thinking about how I didn't get a chance to truly take in our Christmas Eve together. After I woke up late Christmas day, I was in my bed, alone, and he was gone. He'd left me to pick up the pieces of everything he'd shattered. After getting myself together, having a shower and slipping in some Christmas pajamas to spend the holiday alone, my dad turned up unannounced, demanding answers about where I had been. He was fucking furious.

After some time, I managed to spin a story that I was left stranded and he made me take him to my car, which luckily, was still there. He asked about Blaise, and I told him that I didn't want to see him anymore. He tried to convince me otherwise, as always. Said he was a good man and all that bullshit, but I saw different. Blaise is a grade A cunt, and I don't want to see him ever again. Especially after smacking him over the head with a frying pan.

Eventually, my dad agreed. But even though I feel some ease right now—like he's off my back and I'm not being forced to be with Blaise—Rook still looms in the back of my mind, like a dark cloud. His touch still burns hot on my skin, his claim too deep for me to scrub away. He's all I think and dream about, more than ever, and nothing I do can change it. I know this will take time. So much time. Losing someone you love, whether it's through death or just... being gone, is a process.

But this past week, I've done something I never thought I would—I've been trying to find ways to be with Rook, freely, even though I know deep down it's impossible. Every path my heart tries to take is blocked by a fucking tombstone—my dad.

So tonight, if I'm brave enough, I'll finally tell him the truth about how I feel about Rook. I haven't really said it before, not even once, because just mentioning his name has been shaky ground since he caught us. I know his reaction will be explosive, and that scares the shit out of me. But I can't keep holding on, can't keep pretending. I can't keep living like this.

I'm hoping that, if he hears it from my lips—his daughter, his only child—maybe, just maybe, he'll see that Rook is who I want.

Unless, of course, I've already lost Rook. Which, there's always that big possibility.

I sigh and get to my feet, forcing my body to walk toward my wardrobe. I pick out a black, elegant dress and a matching pair of heels, tossing them onto the bed. My dad will expect me to be glammed up to the nines to parade me around no doubt.

Chapter Fifteen

When I'm ready, I face the mirror. My makeup is flawless, my long black hair curled perfectly, but none of it matches how dead I feel inside tonight. My fists tighten at my sides, rage simmering beneath the surface, and before I can stop myself, I grab a packet of makeup wipes from the desk. I tear a few free and scrub at my face, wiping away the layers until there's nothing left—no foundation, no lipstick, no mask. Just skin.

I grab my hairbrush, dragging it through the curls until they fall into messy waves. My heels hit the floor with a sharp kick, and I don't hesitate as I rip the tight dress off my body, throwing it aside. My steps are quick and purposeful as I storm toward the wardrobe, pulling out a simple oversized black t-shirt, a cropped leather jacket, and a pair of black tights. I grab my boots and sit on the edge of the bed to put everything on.

Once I'm dressed, I stand and turn back to the mirror, staring at the reflection looking back at me.

No fancy dress. No heels. No perfect hair. No layers of makeup and false eyelashes.

This is me.

The real fucking me that I keep burying, hiding away just to keep everyone else happy.

Except one person. *Rook.*

His deep words echo in my mind: *"You don't always have to be flawless, Bunny. You don't have to always be perfect—to be perfect to me."*

My eyes well up again, tears threatening to fall, but I force them back with a deep, steady inhale. A new wave of willpower washes over me as I square my shoulders, turning toward the door.

Noel of Sin

When I step out of the cab in front of my dad's mansion, the place is alive with energy. Snow still clings to the edges of the driveway, melting under the glow of lights and the rumble of engines. I stare ahead, watching people pour through the doors, the base of music vibrating in the air even from here as luxurious motorbikes line the street. I take a shaky breath, readying myself, and move forward.

Inside, the chaos swallows me whole. People are drinking, laughing, and grinding to the music, the air thick with sweat and the smell of liquor. Bikers party hard—I've known this my whole life—but all I care about is making it to the kitchen to pour myself a strong drink.

I weave through the crowd, dodging elbows and sidestepping spilled drinks until, finally, I reach the kitchen. It's surprisingly empty compared to the rest of the house, a small pocket of calm amidst the madness. A few people nod as I pass, but I barely acknowledge them. My focus is on the counter.

I grab a cup and a bottle of whiskey, my hands steady despite the adrenaline coursing through me. Pouring a shot, I throw it back in one swift motion. The burn hits instantly, scorching my throat and making me cough, but it's exactly what I need.

"Ebony?" my deep dad's voice cuts through the noise behind me, loud and unexpected. "Why aren't you dressed? You're…"

I spin around to face him, my pulse quickening, but the words die in my throat as my world shrinks, my gaze locking onto one figure in the haze of people behind him—Blaise.

A flash of anger rushes through me, but I snap out of it as soon as my dad steps forward, gesturing at my outfit with his hand. His expression changes: he's disappointed, but I glance down at myself as the room around me blurs.

"I like it," I say flatly, almost robotic, my voice void of emotion.

He stops in his tracks, his jaw tightening as he studies me. The tension between us is already brewing, thickening the air, I can feel it creeping around my spine, tightening, but I push through it, lifting my chin and moving my eyes back to Blaise. He's standing there, glass of whiskey in hand, his tattooed fingers wrapped around it like a taunt, staring at me.

"What's he doing here?" I demand, shooting a pointed look at my dad.

My dad side-eyes Blaise for a moment, but his gaze quickly returns to mine. "Listen, Ebony—"

"No, Dad," I snap, my voice cracking like a whip as I cut him off.

Then, my eyes squeezing shut, my heart pounding wildly in my chest. When I open them again, his expression is stunned, like I've just smacked him.

"I am not fucking being with—" I jab a finger in Blaise's direction— "that."

Blaise smirks, lifting his glass and taking a small sip, his eyes glinting with amusement, like he's enjoying every second of this disaster.

"You'll do as you're told," my dad bites as his face flushes a deep, angry red.

Blaise steps forward now, and I feel my body tense instinctively.

"You made it just in time," he says as his gaze moves over my outfit, taking it all in.

"In time for what?" I ask, confusion flickering across my face.

Blaise doesn't answer right away. Instead, he reaches into his pocket, pulling something out and when I see it, my stomach drops, and my eyes widen in disbelief. He flips open the lid, revealing a sparkling diamond ring that glints cruelly under the light.

"It's our engagement party," Blaise sneers.

My breath hitches, and my eyes snap to my dad's. Tears well up instantly as I shake my head, my plea quiet but desperate.

"No—"

"You'll do as you're told, Ebony," my dad repeats, his tone colder now, more final.

"NO, I WON'T!" I shout as my anger flares, wild and uncontrollable, and it makes him straighten, his jaw clenching.

"I'm not marrying that piece of shit! You can't make me—I'm done!"

I move to push past him, but his hand snaps out, grabbing my upper arm with a brutal grip and yanking me back.

"Ebony!" he growls, the warning in his tone echoing through me, but all I see is red.

"Fuck you, Dad! I fucking hate you!" The words rip out of me, my chest heaving with rage. "How can you do this to me? Your own daughter!"

"Because it's for your best interest!" he fires back.

"MY best interest?" I scoff. "You mean YOUR best interest."

For a moment, we're locked in a battle of furious stares, his eyes blazing with fury while mine overflow with defiance.

"You don't give a fuck about me!" I croak, the words spilling out now, unfiltered, unstoppable. "This isn't about me—it's about business. You're willing to sell your own fucking daughter off for a deal."

His chest heaves, his lips part to say something, but I cut him off.

"Mom would never have allowed this. She would have fucking killed your ass for destroying her daughter's life!"

He loses it suddenly, his hand striking my face with such force that my head whips to the side, my hair falling like a curtain over my stinging cheek. The sharp, metallic taste of blood fills my mouth, and before I can even think, his fingers grip my face harshly, forcing me to look at him.

Tears stream down as I breathe harshly, my chest heaving while his face is inches from mine, his eyes burning with anger.

"Don't ever talk about your mother like that in front of me again," he growls. "This is about your future. Your fucking kids' future. Put your selfish, childish bullshit aside and stop living in your little bubble for once. This is reality, princess."

I don't say a word, and his grip tightens for a second, then his voice drops to a near whisper.

"You have no future with him, Ebony. He can't give you what you need. You know that don't you? It's all a fantasy. That little cunt is lucky I haven't blown his kneecaps off with my shotgun already. He's lucky I love his mom. But love?" He sneers, his breath hot and whiskey infused against my face. "Love isn't always enough. Not when it comes to my daughter."

I don't need him to say the name—I already know he's talking about Rook.

"You keep this shit up, keep defying me for him, and I'll do what I've always wanted to do." His grip loosens slightly, his tone chillingly casual now. "I'll end him. It's your fucking choice. Choose wisely."

With that, he shoves my face away and turns, walking off as if nothing happened. I stand there, frozen for a moment, my whole-body rigid. Slowly, I wipe the blood from the corner of my mouth with the back of my hand before Blaise steps closer, looming over me like a shadow.

I refuse to meet his eyes. Instead, I move to walk away, but his hand clamps down on my arm and the touch sends a jolt of disgust through me, but I don't stop to think. I try to yank my arm free and spin around, shooting him a glare so sharp it could shatter glass.

"Don't touch me, motherfucker," I seethe.

Blaise's lips curve into a smug grin as he leans in. "Where are you going, princess? I'm proposing to you in five minutes."

I tilt my chin, raising a eyebrow. "I'd rather fucking die than be with a prick like you. I'm leaving."

I turn sharply, determined on storming off, but his hand grips my arm again, yanking me back. Before I can spit another insult, he presses his phone to my ear. His dark eyes bore into mine as I listen, the pounding bass of the music fading into the background.

At first, I don't register the sound—but then it hits me. It's me, moaning, breathless. Then Rook's voice follows, deep and unmistakable. Finally, my voice again, gasping his name.

My blood turns to ice.

Blaise pulls the phone away and tucks it smoothly into his pocket.

"I think you understand now," he says. "You're not dumb, are you?"

My body shakes with barely contained rage, my chest rising and falling.

"Just accept the proposal, Ebony, and I won't tell your daddy how you spent Christmas night fucking your own brother. Then, Rook doesn't die."

A tear glides down my cheek, burning hot against my skin. My mind races, piecing it together—the stupid hairclip he gave me. It must have had a recording device. He set me up.

But why?

Blaise's fingers brush over my wet, bruised cheek, his touch sickeningly tender and I jerk back instinctively, but his grasp tightens on my arm.

"Don't worry, sweetheart," he breathes. "I'm gonna take real good care of my fiancée. I'm taking you home tonight to solidify our engagement. You won't escape me twice."

His gaze lingers on my face a moment longer, relishing my torment, before he finally releases me and strides off.

As soon as he's gone, my breath comes in shallow gasps, my chest tight as my vision blurs with tears. My thoughts spiral, panic clawing at me as I watch Blaise and my dad talking in the distance, their figures blurring in the haze of the crowd.

An uncontrollable sob escapes me, tearing through my chest and I feel defeated—trapped. But then, something inside me snaps.

I won't do this anymore.

Without another glance back, I stride through the crowd, my steps quickening as I head for the garage door. When I enter, I hit the button on the wall to open the shutters, the hum of the machinery barely reaching my ears.

My hands tremble as I snatch a set of keys off the hook before I climb onto a sleek black motorbike, jamming the key into the ignition. The engine roars to life, the sound rumbling in my chest. Kicking up the stand, I grip the handlebars tightly and gun it forward, flying out onto the now rainy street.

The cold, wet wind tears at my hair as I leave the mansion—and the monsters inside it—far behind.

Noel of Sin

As I ride, countless of memories with Rook flood through my mind. One after the other like a video reel.

The warm summer evenings in the pool, just me and him. The way he used to throw me into it, almost drowning me. But to be honest, now I think about it, I believe he only did it because he wanted to see if my tits would flop free from my bikini.

Those times I would get tired of studying, so I would sneak into his bedroom late at night, curl up on his lap as he was sitting in his gaming chair, my head tucked beneath his chin and read a book while he gamed on his computer till the early hours of the morning.

That one spring he whisked me away when I had an argument with my dad about not being able to ride a motorbike when I wanted to, but he refused to teach me because I was a girl. Rook made it his mission to teach me, because girls can ride bikes too. He spent hours with me making sure I'd never forget how to ride one.

After what feels like forever, I pull off at the side of a dark, empty road, the bike skidding slightly on the slick pavement as it comes to a stop. The night is bare, the only sound the relentless drum of rain against the world around me. Water streams down my face and hair, mingling with tears I can't hold back, soaking through my thin clothes and leaving me shivering on the bike.

My legs shake as I reach into my jacket, fumbling to pull out my phone, my fingers are stiff from the cold. The screen lights up, casting a pale glow over my face as I stare down at it, my chest rising and falling with shallow, panicked breaths.

His name is right there. Rook.

My thumb hovers over the screen, but I can't press it. Not yet. Everything smashes down on me—what I've done, what I've left behind. Blaise will tell my dad. He'll show him the recording. It's already too late. Just do it, Ebony. Do what's right for you for once, I tell myself. I take a sharp breath, forcing my thumb to move, pressing the call button.

The phone rings.

Each tone slices through the night like a cruel reminder of everything I've lost. It rings again, then again, and still, no answer.

My heart races, a frantic beat against my ribcage. The rain feels heavier now, colder, as my hopes sink deeper with every passing second. I press the phone harder against my ear, praying, *please, Rook, pick up, please.*

But nothing.

When the call finally cuts off, my heart shatters and I pull the phone away, staring at the screen as it fades back to the call log. My hands tremble so badly I almost drop it. Tears blur my vision as I open our message thread.

[Please, Rook. I need you.]

The words are barely readable through watery eyesight, but I hit send anyway, feeling like it's the only bit of control I have left. I send the five-word message before squeezing my phone in my hand.

For a moment, I sit there in the rain, clutching the phone to my chest, as sobs tear through me. I glance back the way I came, the dread pressing tighter now. Blaise, my dad—they'll come after me. But none of it matters if Rook doesn't.

But time seems to extend, and I break down completely. He's given up on me. I pushed him too far. I've lost him forever. I lower my head onto the handlebars, trying to catch my breath as my weeps come out uneven, until I suddenly hear something in the distance.

I carefully lift my head looking ahead to see a light in the distance heading this way and my heart skips a beat, fearful that it could be my dad or Blaise.

They come quickly, the bikes engine ripping through the silent night and I prepare myself to speed off. When the bike starts to slow down where I am, the front light burning my eyes, but I squint, trying to see who it is. The rain pelts down hard as they stop, dismantling the bike.

When they step in front of the blinding beam, stopping, and clearing my vision, I see it's him.

Rook.

My heart skips a beat, and I jump off the bike instantly, running toward him. As soon as he's close, I jump up, wrapping my arms and legs around him. He catches me and I instantly sob into his shoulder, breaking down.

"I'm so fucking sorry. I should never have let you go the first time," I weep, barely able to get air into my lungs quick enough, my emotions getting the better of me.

His hand finds the back of my neck in a possessive hold as he presses his face into the side of mine, responding in my ear.

"Is that you saying you're ready to be with me now, bunny?"

I lift my head, my fingers weaving through the back of his dark, wet hair and I look into his green eyes.

"Yes," I say quietly.

His forehead rests against mine as he looks down, taking a moment before his gaze lifts to mine, searching.

"You know what this means, don't you?"

I nod slightly, "I do, and I don't give a fuck if you don't give a fuck." I answer confidently, my breath hot against his lips.

His hand tightens on the back of my neck, pulling me into a kiss that ignites every nerve in my body. The freezing cold rain cascades around us, but I'm too lost in the heat of his lips to care. As we kiss wildly, his hands trail up the back of my cold, drenched thighs, gripping my ass firmly before he starts to move, carrying me with him.

He lowers me onto his bike and his hand slides to the side of my neck. He leans in, capturing my lips again and again, each kiss leaving me breathless.

When he pulls back, his thumb pushing my bottom lip downward, and his green eyes locks onto mine, an unspoken understanding passing between us. We stare at each other, the intensity in his gaze mirroring my own.

This is it.

We're together now, and while the battles ahead may be far from over, I know we'll fight to the death to hold on to what we have from now on.

"Let's get the fuck out of here," Rook says, before he swings onto the bike in front of me, his movements swift and sure.

My arms wrap tightly around his waist as I press into his warmth, finally feeling a moment of peace in the storm. The engine growls beneath us, and with a surge of power, he takes off into the night, the rain blurring the world as we speed away—together.

THE END OF Noel of Sin

Made in United States
Troutdale, OR
05/03/2025